ETHRIA

BY

JASON ARGOS

Vabella Publishing
P.O. Box 1052
Carrollton, Georgia 30112
www.vabella.com

Cover art by Jeskia Barinque. http://sakuyasworld.deviantart.com

13-digit ISBN 978-1-942766-15-5

Library of Congress Control Number 2016908967

10 9 8 7 6 5 4 3 2 1

For T.L. Gray

Thank you for believing in me.

PROLOGUE

Five years ago…

"Sir, we have to fall back!"

Streaks of auburn light flashed across a starless sky as pulse rifles discharged rounds of ionized energy. Flashes of bright yellow lit up the heavens, giving a seconds warning before a tank's ion cannon pulverized another building, sending a fresh batch of soldiers screaming into Death's cold embrace. The bodies of the fallen filled the streets of the once beautiful city of Adom, transforming the ancient metropolis into nothing more than a pile of stone rubble and smoking graves.

"Negative, we complete our objective," the Colonel yelled, dropping an enemy soldier with two quick shots before ducking behind a hill of dirt and stone.

A Sergeant to the Colonel's right shook his head, pressing a hand against an earpiece. "Sir, its suicide to try and advance. Command says enemy reinforcements are inbound."

"Colonel." A young man, wearing a stained gray uniform of an Ethrian Major, scurried over to the older man's side, holding one of his pulse pistols. "Cole and I can get in there."

"That's nuts kid."

Another man, clutching the hilt of his retractable sword, joined them. "If you can cover us, Korso and I could infiltrate the temple and complete the objective."

"Harris, how long till evac?" the Colonel glanced back towards the Sergeant as another cloud of dust and debris exploded into the air.

Eyes wide as he pressed himself lower to the ground, Harris took a quick glance at his watch before looking with a glimmer of hope. "Fifteen minutes."

"You two have ten to get back here, got it?" The Colonel waited long enough to catch their nods before he turned to fire at the enemy. "The rest of you, give them cover fire!"

"You do realize this is probably going to get us killed, don't you?" Cole glanced at his perpetual partner in all things suicidal, ignoring the fresh volley of enemy fire.

"I'm sorry, were you planning on living forever?" Korso smirked, returning his pistol to its holster and drawing his own folding sword.

"Good hunting boys," the Colonel shouted while gesturing towards their target. "Just make sure you get your hides back in time to catch our ride."

Korso and Cole sprinted towards the temple while the rest of their squadron laid down suppression fire, weaving between whatever cover they could find to avoid the searing rounds of incoming energy. Reaching the entrance to the stone cathedral, they each extended the blades of their swords with an all too familiar metallic ring, cutting down a pair of enemy soldiers without breaking stride. Darting through dusty, vine covered corridors; they descended deeper into the ancient structure. Dust and small chunks of stone fell in waves while the sound of canon fire reverberated through the halls. Dropping down a series of golden stairs, the duo found a tall, middle aged man in brown armor sitting in front of a golden statue.

"Raj!" Korso slid to a stop.

"It's time you died." Cole's face hardened as he began to circle around the enemy commander.

"Yes, it may be, but I am ready for death." Raj stood and turned to face them, drawing a heavy broadsword with a slow deliberate motion. “Killing me will not win this war. It shall only slow the progress of our new order. You cannot stop the inevitable.”

“The hell we can’t,” Korso stated, readying his sword. “We have a knack for doing what can't be done.”

“Some say it’s rather annoying. But even if what you say is true, then we will gladly die trying,” Cole replied.

Raj nodded with a slight laugh. “So be it.”

* * *

Two years later…

“It is my honor to bestow upon you, Alexander Korso, the title of Seraph Prime and Supreme Commander of the imperial armies of Ethria.” Emperor Michael Serra pinned a blue and gold medal onto Korso’s crisp white uniform before placing a hand on his shoulder. “The burden I give is great, but there is no one I trust more to carry it.”

“Thank you, your majesty.” Korso bowed.

Watching Korso play to the crowd along with the Emperor from a palace balcony, Cole fought back the urge to unleash a plasma round into everyone gathered in the grassy square and settled for a discreet roll of his eyes. “I fought in the same battles he has, and yet *he* is chosen to be Seraph Prime while I rise no higher than a common place Colonel.”

Anton Chaple, a tall, clean shaven man, nodded in his usual stiff fashion. “Great men are often over looked until years after their war has ended.”

“Korso is the soldier the Empire needs.” Cole let out a slight laugh, keeping his gaze on the scene below. “But the Emperor lacks vision. When this war is over, I will assume the role that should have been mine.”

CHAPTER ONE

Now…

The *Sprinthawk*, a twenty-five meter long light freighter, cruised past the second of three moons orbiting the planet Ethria. Metallic gray, save for a few dark blue sections of the hull, its angled surfaces were mostly unbroken except for where the hull met the tinted canopy of the cockpit. By all appearances, the faceted ship looked like any other small freighter, by design of its Captain, until she bore her teeth and revealed herself as an Eagle-class warship.

Ethria had a light green sky and was still considered a forest plant despite the generations of development and hyper mechanized cities that filled the nine major continents.

"You know, Dee, I really can't tell you how much I hate the dress whites," Korso complained, fidgeting in his white and blue dress uniform and the vest displaying the medals he earned through years of combat service.

"It is customary for the Seraph Prime to wear such a uniform," Dee replied in his typical stoic manner. Older than Korso by ten years and twice his size—all of it being muscle—Dee wore a uniform similar to Korso's, but instead of being white, his was dark green. Several inches taller than Korso, Dee spoke with a deep voice, one that somehow managed to both sooth and intimidate. "Also, it is customary for one to dress up when they are going to meet with the Emperor."

"The Emperor wanted to see me, not the other way around." Korso pulled the controls to the right, flying the ship past the third moon and began his entry into the atmosphere. "We just spent three months babysitting the final negotiation of the peace treaty with the Klayvor. Before that we were at war for eight years. Now I finally get to go home and what happens? The Emperor wants to meet us so he can give us some lame medal of valor."

"Most people would be honored to receive such a medal." Dee shook his shaved head, giving Korso a disapproving glance.

"We each have two." Korso shot Dee an annoyed glare and ran a hand over his short brown hair before returning his attention to piloting the ship over the capital city and landing in the royal hanger.

"True, but that is not the only reason we were asked to see the Emperor."

"And that's what's got me so pissed off. After all we've been through; he wants us to be bodyguards for the Princess, whom I've never met."

"As Seraph Prime, you were tasked with protecting the Empire. Is it not also an honor to be asked to protect that which is most precious to the Emperor?"

"I love the old man as much as you, but—" Korso brought the ship to a slow crawl, sending his identification code to port control. "—no. I'm not feeling the honor. If he wants to honor me, he can name a wing of the palace after me, *after* I go home."

* * *

"The damage was minor, majesty, but had they reached any further..."

Tuning out the dry, cracking voice of the gray haired advisor speaking with the Emperor, Cole glanced over the light gray walls of the throne room, wondering how long it must have taken to carve the golden symbols into the marble. The spacious chamber allowed plenty of room for any large ceremony or presiding, while still conveying a sense of power and superiority in whoever sat on the throne. Even the tiled floor lent to the allure of greatness, reflecting light from the tinted windows in such a way that gave whoever sat on the throne an almost god like radiance.

Chaple stood to Cole's right, clean cut as ever, wearing a military style gray suit with his hands clasped behind his back. "I believe we should strike now if we are to keep the element of surprise."

"I concur." Cole nodded, jealous of the impassive man's attire. As head of the Ethrian Defense Ministry, Cole felt it was important to wear the black and red uniform of the EDM. It conveyed the message that their leader fought in the trenches alongside them, that he would still get his hands dirty, and that he understood what they went through. It was a simple tactic, one that made keeping the loyalty of his people easier. It showed humility in his duties; which was exactly the image he wanted the public to see. "Your majesty, such an insult must not be tolerated."

"We have no proof that the T'loak are responsible for the attack on Sentinel," the Emperor growled, waving a stubby fingered hand. "We have just ended a war. I see no reason to start a new one."

"That is precisely why I should rule." Cole let a cold edge line his words.

The Emperor turned toward him, wearing an incredulous look on his pale, withered face. "What?"

"You lack foresight. Did you know that all throughout the wars, I was one of the most feared weapons you had at your disposal? I was feared because I did what needed to be done to ensure victory. I conquered worlds in your name, only to learn that you lack the will to properly wield the power I enabled you to gain." Cole locked his gaze on the Emperor's wide eyes while thumbing the switch that sent his sword unfolding with a metallic ring. "Rest assured, Majesty, that as ruler of the Empire, I will have no qualms about the *proper* exercising of power."

"This is treason!"

"Yes it is, but it's for the greater good." Cole pointed the tip of his sword at the Emperor's neck.

"You cannot do this," the adviser stated, panic twisting his face.

"Obviously, I can." Cole smiled, swinging his sword and slashing the old man's throat. He then turned back to the Emperor

and plunged his blade into the Emperor's chest. Twisting his sword free as he shoved the lifeless body to the floor, Cole took a long, satisfied breath, watching as the Emperor's blood stained the dark gray tile. "The Emperor is dead."

"Long live the Emperor." Chaple bowed.

"This was all so avoidable." Cole knelt over the body of the Emperor and shook his head, surprised at how much regret churned his stomach.

"My Lord?"

"Replacing the stained tile is going to be rather expensive." Cole let out an amused laugh, but the hiss of a door sliding open drew his attention to the right side of the chamber, and the Princess.

Staggering into the chamber, her pretty, twenty six year old face twisted in horror, she looked from Cole and his associate to her father's body. "Dad?"

"Oh, my dear Princess, what have you done?" Cole smirked, wiping some of the blood off of his sword.

"What?" Rachael staggered back, her face pale as she sucked in air in short, jagged breaths.

"Such a cruel girl, killing her own father just to gain the throne." Cole stepped toward the red haired woman, relishing the anguish and panic in her emerald eyes. "Kill her."

"At your pleasure, my Lord," Chaple replied, a moment before the Princess turned and ran through the door.

* * *

The corridors of the royal palace were lined with a pristine, white marble, giving them a hygienic appearance, while lavish tapestries hung from the ceiling. The floors, tiled with a golden brown sandstone, magnified every step Korso and Dee took as they made their way through the corridors.

"So after we've politely refused the Emperor, our lives become painfully simple. So how does Damascus Dee, retired Lt. Colonel of the Ethrian army, plan to spend his days?" Eager to finish his business with the Emperor, Korso turned down another corridor, mulling over all the unimportant pleasantries he missed from his civilian life. Glancing towards the older man, Korso half expected one of Dee's infamous *I haven't decided yet* shrugs, when the sound of shouting and boots running on tile drew his attention.

"What is that?" Dee asked, tilting his head.

Before Korso could speculate an answer, a young woman—dressed in red and white with gold trim—bolted into the corridor with five men wearing EDM uniforms and a man clad in gray on her heels.

Crashing into Dee, the woman's face flashed a hint of relief before peering over her shoulder. "Dee, you've gotta help me. He killed him..."

"Who the hell is this and why does it sound like she has the entire palace guard chasing after her?" Korso peered at the sword wielding men that had followed the woman, noting the approach of more footsteps.

"What has happened?" Dee asked.

"Keep running Princess and you'll only die tired." Cole stepped into the corridor and pushed past his men, smiling as his gaze met Korso's. "Well, this is an unexpected surprise. I wasn't aware of your return, Korso. You saved me the trouble of tracking you down."

"Cole, what the hell is going on?" Confusion choking his thoughts, Korso glanced from Cole to the woman growling at Dee's side. "Did you say Princess?"

"Forgive me. Since you just arrived on planet, I'll fill you in. You and Princess Rachael conspired to kill the Emperor and seize the throne for yourselves. A most heinous act of betrayal; however, while attempting to escape, the now acting Seraph Prime, *me*, was forced to kill the both of you." Cole flashed a seditious grin. "And with the two of you dead, succession of the throne naturally falls to me."

"Why… why would you do this?" Mind reeling, Korso stared wide eyed at the blond haired man in disbelief, desperate to find how he was misreading the situation. "Why?"

Cole let out an amused chuckle as he stiffened his shoulders and slid his hands behind his back. "You're usually so quick with a snappy response, but now all you can mutter is why? You of all people must understand my reasons."

"How could you betray a man you spent eight years fighting for?" Disbelief shifting to anger, Korso held his gaze on his longtime friend, hoping to find some hint of the man he fought, bled, and nearly died with. "How could you betray *me*?"

"Everything I do, I do for the good of Ethria." The amused look fell from Cole's face, replaced by a cold, unforgiving scowl, one Korso had seen many times. One reserved for the opponents he intended to crush. "I am a patriot, one serving the Empire I fought to protect from a cancerous weakness that would lead to its destruction. I would have asked you join me, but we both know you're too mired in the doctrine of Emperor Michael Serra. Still, you and I have been through quite a lot. I could use you at my side."

"What about the current Emperor?" Korso asked, fearing the answer.

"The Emperor was always a bit of a klutz." Cole shrugged. "As such, it seems he took a nasty fall, onto my sword."

"Murdering Bastard!" Rachael reached for her sword only to have Dee grab her arm.

"What do you say Korso?" Cole held out his arms. "Fight by my side again. Help me protect the world we both love. When we're together, there is no power in this galaxy that can defeat us."

Korso shook his head, bottling up the emotions tearing away at his insides. "You know I won't."

"I figured as much." Cole let out a disappointed sigh, closing his blue eyes. "But we all must sacrifice for the good of the Empire, and I can't have you running around. I have an Empire to rebuild."

Still holding onto the Princess's arm, Dee pulled her behind him and leaned closer to Korso. "We are at an extreme disadvantage and without our weapons. It would be best if we retreated to the ship."

"I can get us out of here," Rachael exclaimed, starting down the corridor with Dee.

"This ain't over, Cole." Korso spun around, sprinting after them.

"Kill them." Cole's voice reverberated off the marble walls.

Letting his outrage fuel his legs, Korso raced down a wide corridor, instinct sending a hand to search for a pistol he didn't have. Cursing at the screech of the palace alarm, he veered left, still questioning if he had somehow misread the situation. Maybe it was all a dream. Some twisted nightmare developed by his enemies to drive him mad. He wanted to believe that, but the terror surging through his gut felt all too familiar; too real.

"Stop!"

His attention snapping back to reality, Korso looked up just as one of the three guards ahead loosed a plasma round, heating the air as it sailed passed his head. Diving into a corridor to avoid another plasma round, he rolled to his feet, ignoring the string of rifle fire flashing behind him and spotted Dee and the Princess running ahead. "There goes our way back to the Hawk, and we'll be boxed in if we go the long way."

"I know another way." Rachael peered over her shoulder, veering into another columned hall. "Come on."

Shooting past a large stained window, Korso glanced behind him, counting nine guards plus the man in gray pursuing them. He knew they had a narrow window to elude capture, assuming of course Cole hadn't already boxed them into a trap, but Korso fought back his fear, knowing it would do little good. He had been in hopeless situations before, often surrounded by enemy forces and had lived to embellish the tale. Of course, he had always been armed and those enemies had never been his own people before.

Rachael turned left, bursting through a pair of double doors and led them into a large wood paneled room. "Block the door."

"You think?" Korso shot her a quick glare and scanned the sunlit room. Grabbing one of the many plush wooden chairs sitting around a large mahogany table, he turned and slid it under the doors handle just as Dee slammed them closed. He motioned towards the table and lifted one end while Dee grabbed the other and tilted it on its side before pushing it against the doors.

"That will not hold for long." Dee backed away, looking over the chamber.

"I know." Korso spun around, taking in the room. There were a few large windows filtering sunlight on the wall to the right, and a number of paintings decorated the walls, but no other doors. "Great job Princess, we're trapped in a dining hall."

"Did you have a better plan?" Rachael moved along the left wall, running her hands over an ivory column.

Korso growled, searching for anything he could use as a weapon. "It'll take them all of two minutes to figure out where we are. If I'm going to die, I'd rather die swinging. Not shot in a dining room."

"You'll have your chance in a moment." Dee moved away from the door.

"Or…" Rachael moved her hand, revealing a coin sized scanner. An instant later, Korso caught the sound of a hydraulic hiss as one of the wooden panels slid back, uncovering a dark passageway. "You can shut up and go this way."

"Fair enough." Korso hurried after the Princess, ducking into the narrow passage behind Dee.

"This can get us down to the hanger," Rachael stated over the hiss of the panel closing.

"I never knew these tunnels existed," Dee replied, forced to crouch low as he walked.

"My great grandfather was a bit paranoid from what I hear, and had the tunnels added when he renovated the palace." Rachael glanced over a shoulder, her face cloaked in darkness. "I used them to sneak around as a kid. No one knew about them, except for me and my… my dad."

Stepping past one of the few yellow emergency lights placed in ten yard intervals that kept them from moving in total darkness, Korso let out a breath, remembering his time spent joking with the Emperor. "I didn't know about them, so hopefully Cole doesn't either."

Following Rachael through the weaving series of passages, they worked their way to the port unnoticed, and emerged in a large, unlit storage closet. Korso hurried over to the silver door and peaked out as he pushed it open. Not seeing any security forces, the trio hurried towards the *Sprinthawk*, but the sound of a shouting woman wearing an EDM uniform drew his attention.

"Guess Cole's done playing." Korso punched in the access code for the entry hatch and pushed the heavy door open. Waiting as Dee and the Princess entered, he slammed the hatch closed and sprinted to the cockpit.

"We've got to get out of here." Rachael sat in the pilot's chair.

"Hold up Princess." Korso grabbed her by the arm and yanked her out of his chair. Starting up the main system, he strapped himself in, powering up the sub-light engines. "No one flies my ship but me or Dee, got it? And since he's bringing shields and weapons online, you can sit at the comm station or in the hold."

"The hanger doors are still closed." Dee's hands flew across the panel to Korso's left, bringing power to the ships secondary functions with an all too familiar tension and focus.

"Luckily, we have the access codes." Korso grabbed the controls as the maneuvering thrusters fired up, making the ship hover over the guards rushing towards them while turning it around.

"How could you have the codes?" Rachael strapped herself into the chair behind Dee. "They're only issued with a cleared departure, which Cole is sure to have blocked."

"He means we're going to blow the doors open." Dee fired a single concussion missile, blasting apart the hanger doors in a blaze of orange fire and dust.

Punching the main thrusters, Korso flew the *Sprinthawk* out of the hanger, ignoring the shrill cries from the port control coming in over the comm. Clearing the atmosphere as rapidly as he could without causing a burnout, he veered the ship away from the moons, scanning for any comm traffic about their escape. After a moment of listening, he checked the sensors, surprised that no one was following them.

"Umm, we're being hailed." Rachael peered down at the console in front of her.

"Are we now?" Korso stood and flipped the switch that activated the holo-projectors. A moment later, an image of Cole shimmered into existence. "What no EDM fleet to see me off?"

"I've already dispatched someone to pursue you more quietly. I wouldn't want to create a panic," Cole stated, cold distain seething in his voice. "Honestly, how long do you think you can run? I will kill all of you and become the one *true* Emperor of Ethria."

Rachael jumped to her feet, her face twisted and red with rage. "Over my dead body."

The image of Cole flickered as he let out a callous laugh. "Of course, I wouldn't have it any other way. And I'll hunt you across the galaxy if I have to."

"You're forgetting one thing, Cole. Never hunt what you can't kill." Anger and betrayal adding a dangerous edge to his voice,

Korso cut off the transmission. Forcing himself to take a breath, he stepped over to the helm and changed their course.

"Where are we heading?" Dee turned to face him.

"We need fuel. There's a small space station a few systems over where we can get some supplies and figure out our next move," Korso explained.

"I know that station, and it's a total dive." Rachael sat back in her chair. "Besides, it's really not the smartest of ideas to stay close to this system."

"We don't have a choice, unless you plan to get out and push the ship." Korso shot the Princess a cross look while turning to leave. "We stop there but we keep it short. It won't take Cole long to find us if we linger."

CHAPTER TWO

Having spent most of the hour flight sitting alone, trying to find some logical reason for Cole's actions, Korso returned to the bridge wearing his usual midnight blue and black fatigues with plenty of concealed pockets. He carried two custom made silver pulse pistols, one in each thigh holster, with the hilt of his folding sword attached to his black belt.

Finding the Princess talking with Dee, Korso stepped towards her holding a large cloth bag. "Here you are Princess, found some clothes for you. Looks like they'll fit you."

"What's wrong with what I'm wearing?" Rachael turned towards him, her eyes narrowing into a glare.

"You mean other than the fact that dressing like a member of the royal family makes you stand out like a vibrant krell in a school full of mangled lumas."

Rachael scowled at him for a long moment, clearly biting back some comment, before snatching the bag from his hand and marching out. "Fine."

Korso sat in the copilot's seat while Dee began docking the ship to the cylindrical station. Waiting until he finished, Korso smirked, noting that Dee had changed into a pair of dark green fatigues. "No medals? You seemed so proud to wear them."

"I thought it prudent to remove them, at least while we are here." Dee returned his smirk as he stood. "Besides, I would hate to make you look bad. The uniform does look better on me, after all."

"Keep dreaming baldy." Korso followed Dee down to the port side hatch and found Rachael waiting. "So they fit?"

"It's a little tight." Rachael attached her red and gold sword hilt to her slate gray belt.

"Well you're a bit taller and more… developed than the last girl to wear them." Korso looked over the Princess, surprised by how nice the sleeveless lavender flight suit complemented her slender figure.

"Hey, eyes up here." Rachael snapped her fingers. "Why do you even have these?"

"Because." Ignoring her irate response, Korso opened the hatch and stepped out into the station hanger where they were greeted by a pudgy, lime scaled, four foot tall Beewa male with a crude cybernetic arm.

"Welcome to Blue Haven." The man spoke in a forced cheerful tone typical of the Beewa. "How long do you plan on staying with us? Daily port fees are the equivalent of five hundred units of galactic standard currency."

"We'll just be here a couple hours." Korso surveyed the layers of grime covering the rust colored walls, growing more and more eager to depart.

"Very well sir. Please access our online systems if you require anything." The pudgy male entered a few notes into his genpad before turning his angular eyes towards Korso's weapons. "Forgive me sir, but station policy forbids the presence of any firearms. I am afraid you will have to return your guns to your ship or check them into a secured locker until you depart."

"You wanna take his gun but not our swords?" Rachael glanced down at the Beewa.

"Standard procedure on most stations. Wouldn't want some drunken yahoo to blow out a window or puncture the hull, killing everyone on board." Korso handed his pistols to Dee. "I'll cheek out the station and see about getting some supplies delivered."

"I'll see to refueling then," Dee replied

Korso stepped past the Beewa with Rachael close behind him, and made his way into the station. Weaving their way through the swarming station, they found the trade district, a shabby collection of exorbitantly priced shops filled with beings from multiple worlds, and settled on the least dingy looking one to purchase what they needed.

"That's ridiculous." Rachael glared across the counter at a gangly woman. "Your delivery fees are more than what we paid for the supplies."

The woman grunted, playing with a lock of her purple hair. "Swift delivery isn't cheap girl, unless you want to do it yourself."

"It's fine." Korso shot Rachael an angry glare. Figuring that Cole had already frozen his military account by now, he handed the woman a personal account card, one he kept off official channels, hoping that Cole hadn't found it yet.

"Alright, payments gone through." The woman handed Korso back his card. "Your stuff's on its way now."

"Thanks." Korso nodded as he turned and headed back out into the station.

"Why pay that?" Rachael hurried to catch him as he started down the crowded walkways. "We could have found someplace cheaper."

"Not much choice," Korso replied. "Besides, the price might have been a tad lower if you hadn't pissed her off."

"Zhod off."

Spotting a malfunctioning neon sign, Korso stepped around a pair of armored men and turned down another walkway. "Such language, where could you have possibly picked that up, Princess?"

"Wherc are we going?"

"Bar."

"Do we really have time to waste getting drunk?" Rachael shot Korso an annoyed look.

"No, but a few more hours with you and I might feel the need to," Korso replied, matching her glare. "Sadly, that's not why we're going though."

"Then why are we?"

"A piss-hole station like this is going to have a piss-hole tavern filled with let's just say… shady clientele." Korso motioned forward, spotting the bar. "The kind of clientele that always keeps their ears to ground. I'm hoping we can learn something. Any murmurings about what's happening on Ethria are bound to find their way to dumps like these."

Entering the dingy, half lit tavern, Korso tried to block out the scent of rum and a dozen other intoxicants that bombarded his senses. Taking a moment to look over the bustling room, he walked over to the bar and sat on one of the stained stools while Rachael took the seat next to him. Signaling the bartender, a four armed Hespen male with granite like skin, they each ordered a mug of Ethrian ale.

"Thanks." Korso handed the bartender a sapphire colored coin. Waiting for the Hespen to move on to the next customer, he took a sip from what he could only hope was a clean mug and glanced to his right, surprised to see Rachael chugging hers down like it was water.

"One more," Rachael called to the bartender.

"You're paying for your own you know." Korso took another sip of his own drink.

"Some gentlemen you are," Rachael replied. "Won't even buy a Princess a drink?"

"Well, a lady shouldn't be knocking back ale like an ion cannon goes through coolant."

"I'm no lady."

"I'm gettin' that."

"What's that supposed to mean?" Taking another mug offered by the Hespen, Rachael threw her head back, empting the yellow mug in one long swig. "I can't believe Dee left me with you."

"Until you came running down the hall, my biggest problem was getting another stupid medal. Now, thanks to my apparently

traitorous and oldest friend, half the galaxy is going to think *I'm* a traitor, and I'm stuck here with you, *Princess*."

Rachael shifted her gaze towards him, narrowing her eyes as her face burned red. "Do you always have to have such disdain in your voice when you call me that?"

"I can always call you something else."

"How about using my name, or would that be too much to ask from a military stooge."

"Forgive me *highness*, never meant to offend your delicate sensibilities." Anger lining his voice, Korso finished his ale. "Sorry if this grotesque day has spoiled my mood."

Rachael shot to her feet, her eyes widening for a moment before narrowing into dagger like slits. "You're talking to me about ruined days?"

"Well let's see, there were four people in this galaxy I trusted unequivocally and one of them just murdered the second." Korso stood matching Rachael's glare, unable to hide the anger boiling inside of him.

"You talk about my father like he was a friend."

"He was a friend!"

"And he was my father!" Rachael's face exploded with rage as she shoved Korso back. Eyes watering, she looked away for a long moment before turning back to face him. "I just lost the only person I loved."

Korso let out a long, regretful breath, realizing for the first time that as bad as he felt right now, she had to be feeling a dozen times worse. Running his fingers through his short brown hair, he forced himself to forget about his own anger for the moment and softened his voice. "Look Princess, I'm sorry. I'm sorry for your loss, and I'm sorry if I made it worse. I can't change what happened. All I can do is promise you that I'll do whatever I can to keep you safe, and that Cole *will* answer for what he's done."

"I can take care of myself." Rachael slammed her mug on the bar and stormed off into the crowd.

Good job Korso. Way to comfort a grieving daughter. Korso turned back towards the bar, wishing he could rewind the conversation and try again.

"Man, I tell ya wut." A pale skinned man sat down next to Korso and ordered a honeyed karji. "I'm 'bout ta make me some good coin."

"How's that?" Korso looked over the scared man, noting the unusual amount of knives he carried and the empty holster on his hip. "And who are you?"

"Names Taub, from Gifu in Mino province, and ya ain't heard? There's a rumor dat a huge bounty just came over the net. A fat six billion reward, all in Ethrian currency."

"Six billion, huh?" Korso turned around, searching the room for any sign of danger. "And who's the bounty on?"

"Two Ethrian soldiers and a real pretty Princess. I just hope I find her before everyone else does."

"Everyone else?"

"You know, da other bounty hunters. It is a convention, esca."

"Convention?" Korso forced a smile, trying not choke. "I never knew bounty hunters had conventions."

"Course we do," Taub belched, adding to the aroma of the tavern. "We're an industry like anythin' else. Gots ta stay current wit the latest tech."

"Huh. Excuse me for minute." Korso pushed away from the bar and stepped outside. Reaching into one of his pockets, he pulled out his primary communicator, a three inch rectangular device, and set it to the *Sprinthawk's* frequency. "Dee, you there?"

"I read you," Dee's voice replied.

"We finished refueling and resupplying yet?"

"The provisions you paid for have yet to arrive and the ship hasn't finished refueling."

"Dren," Korso cursed. "Get as much as you can ready to go."

"What has happened?"

"Besides realizing bounty hunters aren't the brightest stars in galaxy; word of our arrival just reached the station." Korso glanced back toward the bar, noticing a few excited shouts and the sound of glass breaking.

"Understood."

Returning the comm to his pocket, Korso hurried back inside, searching for Rachael, and found her fighting with some azure skinned woman. Rachael landed a harsh punch to the woman's jaw an instant before pulling her into a headlock.

"Well done." A man in a gray suit with matching sunglasses stepped out of the crowd, clapping his hands. "However, that is enough fighting for now, my dear Princess."

"You helped murder my father." Rachael's well defined face twisted with fury as she released the woman and shoved her off to the side.

"If you would please come with me, Lord Cole is very anxious see you again," the man stated in a callous voice.

"Well I'm in no rush to see him," Rachael spat.

"Ron, Chu, Fru, please escort the Princess to my ship." Chaple gestured with his left hand.

Moving unnoticed as everyone focused on Rachael and the trio of stocky men in EDM uniforms, Korso weaved his way through the crowd, searching for way to get the Princess and escape.

Hearing the metallic ring of extending weapons, Korso looked up and saw each of the three goons had pulled out a dagger as they charged towards Rachael. Sword springing to life in her hand, Rachael bounded forward, catching the nearest assailant with a slash across the stomach. Parrying an attack from her right, she spun to her left, deflecting a vertical strike with one motion then reversed her swing an instant later, slicing through the second man's jugular. The last man rushed towards her as she turned to face him, but before he could reach her, Korso hurled a heavy bottle of blue ale, knocking the man off his feet as the bottle bounced off the side of his head.

"Tough bottle." Korso plucked the sword off of his belt, releasing its blade while stepping over towards Rachael.

"'Bout time you showed up," Rachael stated, keeping her eyes on Chaple.

"Cole must really want us dead if he sent him after us." Korso stepped over to Rachael, putting a calm mocking note in his voice.

"Lord Cole has promised a great reward for your head, and an even greater one if I bring you back alive." Chaple glanced over to his surviving lackey, unfazed by his men's death.

"Who the zhod is this guy?" Rachael asked.

"He's an assassin working under the Ethrian Defense Ministry." Korso held his weapon ready while slowly pushing Rachael towards the wall behind them.

"Allow me to introduce myself. I am the man who tolls the black bell of death in the name of Emperor Cole, I am Anton Chaple."

Korso flashed an insincere smile as he backed away. "Well it was very underwhelming meeting you in person, but we really should be going."

"I will pay one billion Ethrian credits to whoever brings me those two," Chaple shouted, gesturing towards the retreating duo.

The ambient noise of the curious spectators vanished as the taverns occupants mulled over Chaple's words. An instant later, the entire room erupted, the horde of drunks surging towards Korso and Rachael. Some of the customers started fighting each other while other's tried to grab Rachael or Korso. Lashing out at anyone within striking distance, Korso pulled Rachael towards a large murky window.

"Come on." Korso kicked a lanky man in the chest and grabbed a wooden chair from a nearby table, pitching it through the window.

"Still think this was a good idea?" Rachael leapt through the shattered window a second before Korso and took off down the passageway.

"Just shut up and run." Korso followed a few feet behind Rachael, wishing he had his pistols to thin the horde of pursuing opportunists, as they ran towards the docking bay. Reaching the corridor that led to the docking bay, two men jumped out in front of Rachael. Not slowing, she pushed passed the first man and drove her sword into the second's thick gut, wrenching it free as she continued down the hall. Staring in shock as his partner's blood covered the floor; Korso hammered the second man with a shot to the jaw.

"Dee, get us the hell out of here!" Korso emerged from the corridor tapping the concealed comm within his ear and returned his sword to his hip. Sprinting through the *Sprinthawk's* hatch behind Rachael, he slammed his hand on the control panel, sealing it behind him. Making his way up to the cockpit, he felt the ship pitch to the right as Dee broke away from the station.

CHAPTER THREE

A thousand years ago, mankind left their ancestral homeworld to travel the cosmos and settle other star-systems, a journey that, according to historical logs, took decades. How anyone had ever completed the journey and remained sane was beyond Rachael. After a week of evading every ship, station, or planet that might signal their location to Cole or his assassins, she felt as if she was ready to explode if she didn't get her feet on solid, planetary ground. Of course, those ancient travelers didn't have Korso for a shipmate.

He was infuriating. Always pushing, always poking, always goading her into an argument. Why someone like Dee—a man she had known since she was a child—would choose to fight alongside a dolt like Korso eluded her. Her father had often told her about Korso, admiring the man for his ability to laugh even while staring into the abyss. Her father had an odd sense of humor, one shared by his Seraph Prime, who she had no doubt would happily mouth off to deaths face, if only because he was too stupid to know any better.

Korso had his good points, if only a few. He was helping her to stay alive, despite his childish complaints, and being angry at him kept her from drowning in a torrent grief.

Stepping through the short corridor that led to the cockpit, Rachael found Korso and Dee sitting at the helm. "Where are we?"

"We just entered the Hayfong system," Dee answered.

"Isn't that in T'loak space?" Rachael glanced at Dee, grateful for the invention of inertial dampeners, which kept her from falling on her face as the ship emerged in real-space. "Shouldn't we be staying within our own territory?"

Korso shook his head, looking over the sensors. "Not with the full might of the Ethrian Empire hunting us down."

"Makes sense." Rachael nodded. "But why Hayfong?

"'Cause we can't just wander the galaxy forever." Korso looked up. "The Hayfong system is empty, out of the way, and no one from Ethria would think to look for us here."

Dee gave Korso a skeptical glance. "That is because if an Ethrian is caught in T'loak space, it could start another war."

"So let's not get caught. I figure we can hide here for a while..." Korso pushed a few buttons on the console and brought up an image of a barren, auburn colored planet. "...say on Slovac."

"Is it safe?" Rachael asked.

"Don't know, that's why I'm gonna scout it out first," Korso replied.

"I should accompany you in case you need back up." Dee turned towards Korso.

"Someone has to stay and mind the ship, just in case we need to make another quick exit." Korso stood up, flashing a smirk at Rachael. "Me and the Princess can check it out."

"Very well," Dee said.

Korso led Rachael down to the fairly empty cargo hold and stepped over to a terminal at the base of the narrow stairs. Watching as he entered a few commands, she heard the sound of hydraulic servos as a section of the metal floor plating in the hold's center slid open. A small shuttle, about five meters long with a dark metallic blue hull, ascended out of the hole.

"And what is this?" Rachael paced around the shuttle, noting the emblem of a silver hawk on each side.

"Our ride." Korso stepped over to the craft.

"Is it even space worthy?" Rachael shot him a doubtful look.

"I picked her up on Nautiqa during the war. It was originally an osprey, an underwater recon vessel. After the campaign ended, I had her converted for other uses."

"Why?"

"'Cause it's fast, has a state of the art stealth system, and is great for gathering intel."

"And what do you call it, the *Seahawk*?"

"No… no, that would be… silly." Korso gave an unconvincing shake of his head while opening the sliding hatch. "I wouldn't fly her on a prolonged stellar tour, but she'll be fine to make a planetary drop. So get in already."

"Fine." Rachael smiled, climbing into the seat next him.

Watching as Korso hit a few keys on the center console, Rachael tried to ignore the image flashing through her mind of the craft imploding the instant they hit space. The shuttle lowered back into the hole as Korso grabbed the controls and flew them through a seven meter wide shaft. Clear of the *Sprinthawk*, they cruised down to the planet's barren, rocky surface. Picking up a feint signal as they scanned the sand covered world, Korso landed the shuttle near a pile of rust colored boulders.

"It's hot." Rachael slid the hatch open and climbed out of the shuttle, yearning to stay with the climate controlled craft.

"It's a desert, with twin suns." Korso grabbed a small black remote from the shuttle and hopped out. Scanning the nearby rocks with the remote, he pushed one of the buttons and an image of a boulder formed around the shuttle.

"That standard issue on military crafts?" Rachael waved her hand as a cloud of dust stung her eyes.

"I might have added a few things not purchased through… traditional sources." Korso tucked the remote into a pocket and started towards the large formation of rocks fifty meters ahead of them. "Scans say the signal is coming from underground, probably a cave. Let's see what's inside."

"Any idea whose signal it is?" Rachael followed Korso, spotting the entrance to the caves as they got closer.

"It's not on any military or civilian frequency we use, and I didn't pick up any comm chatter to indicate it belongs to the T'loak."

"Then it's probably smugglers, or slavers, or pirates. All of which can be problems for use."

"Maybe not." Korso paused, reaching the mouth of the cave. "Smugglers and pirates work for money."

"All the more reason to avoid them if they decide to turn us in."

"A nice bribe should solve that problem, and neither group has any love for galactic bodies of authority like Ethria."

"And if they're slavers?" Rachael arched an eyebrow.

"Don't worry Princess, as annoying as you are, I'd never sell you to slavers." Korso grinned, stepping through the narrow opening. "I hate slavers. I'd shoot you first."

"Such a selfless soldier and protector." Rachael rolled her eyes, following after Korso.

Dark, condensed, and muggy, the cave did little to ease Rachael's apprehension. The distinct smell of smoke began to permeate the air the deeper they went. After a short time, the tunnel began to widen as it declined, and grew even muggier with patches of dim, glowing fungus lining the walls. Passing a few large cavities that split off in different passages, they reached a curve in the tunnel and caught the sound of three men talking.

Peering around the corner for a moment, Korso slowly drew one of his pistols as he backed up. "Pretty heavily armed. Maybe we should find another cave."

"Told you this was bad idea." Rachael poked him in the back and turned around, only to find seven soldiers in green and black uniforms, each armed with pulse rifles. "Um… Korso, I think I know whose cave this is."

"Don't move, ginok," one of the soldiers ordered.

"Oh, dren." Korso grabbed Rachael by the arm and pulled her around the corner, only to stop abruptly, causing Rachael to bump into him, as more soldiers blocked their path.

"Surrender or die." A man, dressed in a more ornate version of the soldier's uniform, stepped through the wall of armed men and glared at them with furious brown eyes.

"Was this part of your plan?" Rachael glanced at Korso while four soldiers stepped over to take their weapons.

"Oh shut up," Korso responded.

"Bring them." The man, not much older than Rachael, led them down a series of corridors until they emerged in a large cavern filled with tents, crates, and what looked to be refugees.

"Who are you?" the man demanded, turning to face them while one of the soldiers put their weapons on a large crate.

"I might be the son a millionaire," Korso retorted dryly, only to receive a thumb on the back of the head from a straight faced soldier with short blond hair.

"Be respectful." The blond man stepped over to the leader's side. "Now answer."

"That's the problem with you people, you lack a sense of humor." Korso rubbed the back of his head.

"Wait." Rachael stepped in front of Korso as the blond man raised his weapon to strike again. "You're obviously T'loak, so why not tell us who, specifically, you are?"

The brown eyed man glared at Rachael for a long moment. "I am Von T'naat, crowned Prince of the T'loak."

"Are you here on Cole's orders? Ethrian spies sent to relay our location?" the blond man asked.

"It's irrelevant." Von ran his finger through his black hair, and took a long breath. Gesturing with his right hand, the surrounding soldiers to readied their rifles. "All those who follow my enemy will die."

"Why do I not like where this is going," Korso whispered.

"For crimes against the people of the T'loak, I sentence you to death," Von stated, ice lining his deep voice. "Take them to the fire pits."

"Isn't it customary to hold a trail before sentencing?" Korso struggled to get free as some of the soldiers began to drag them off.

"We're not your enemies," Rachael shouted, panic surging through her as she yanked her arm free.

"Ethrian weapons, Ethrian accents, Ethrian arrogance, and Cole is your Emperor." Von lunged towards her, contempt twisting his scared youthful features.

"No. Cole is *not* our Emperor. He killed my father and took the throne for himself." Rachael matched his stare, refusing to be intimidated. "If you oppose Cole then you and I are on the same side."

"Yeah, the enemy of my enemy…" Korso chipped in.

"And why should I believe you?" Von looked from Korso to Rachael, his posture tense, like a wolf ready to strike.

"Prince Von, if what she says is true, then she is the Ethrian Princess hunted by her own people. If she is telling the truth, then we could trade her to Cole in exchange for a treaty with him," The blonde soldier stated.

"I will not do anything that will aid my enemy, Orrin." Von scowled, glaring at the blond man.

"My apologies, Prince Von."

Von looked back towards Rachael for a moment before turning towards Orrin. "Keep them under guard until I return."

"Yes, my Prince." Orrin bowed as Von strode across the chamber and disappeared into another tunnel.

"Nice try Princess," Korso whispered. "But they're either gonna shoot us and toss our bodies into the fire pits, or they're gonna sell us to Cole. Who will probably have us shot and burn our bodies."

"Your sarcasm isn't helping," Rachael replied, rolling her eyes with a sigh.

* * *

Von walked into a small alcove and stopped in front of a large desk with a few portable computers set up on the smooth surface. A small monitor was attached to the devices, allowing for easier observation and adjustments of the rudimentary security measures he had in place. Switching the system over to communications, he waited, impatiently wishing he could use a more traditional and faster system to communicate rather than waiting for his signal to get bounced off a dozen comm buoys to avoid detection. Finally flashing to life, the screen displayed the image of an older man in an unkempt green and white suit.

"Father." Von bowed his head, noting the bags under his eyes.

"Von, thank the maker you're alright." His father exhaled with a haggard smile.

"Father, I need your advice. Two Ethrians are here, one claiming to be the Princess," Von paused, noticing the faint clouds of dust falling behind his father and the look of concern on his face.

"The Princess is there?"

"Father, What's wrong?"

"Tell me, does she travel with a warrior in blue? The Seraph Prime?"

"Yes, it may be him, but I do not understand. Is she the Princess of Ethria?"

"Yes, but you are in danger. Cole attacks our home even now. He knows that you…" An explosion from behind cut off his father causing the screen to flicker for a moment. When the smoke cleared, Cole stood in what was left of the doorway with three soldiers behind him. "You…"

"Father!" Von reached for the screen out of instinct, hopping to pull his father to safety.

"Prince Von." Cole smiled at the screen holding his bloodied sword. "How nice to see you survived. Now you can watch as your farther dies."

"No," Von shrieked unable to do anything while Cole marched over to his father and plunged his sword through his father's belly. Hands trembling as Cole shoved his father's face into the camera, Von touched the screen, as an icy chill froze his body.

"You have no idea how long I've wanted to do that. Now I need only kill you and the last immediate enemy of Ethria will have fallen." Cole shoved the King's body aside, turning to face one of the soldiers. "Find out where this transmission is coming from."

One of the soldiers stepped over to the computer. "It is coming from the Hayfong system, sixth planet."

"Excellent, I believe Chaple is already near there. Tell him to obliterate everything on the planet." Cole shifted his gaze back to the monitor. "Do give my regards to your father."

Letting out a feral, distraught, cry of rage, Von ripped a silver collapsible spear from the back of his belt and batted the equipment off of the desk as it extended. Wrenching the desk to its side, he smashed the monitor's screen, still showing Cole's image, and turned towards the entrance, unable to keep his eyes from watering.

* * *

Korso sat next to Rachael, leaning with a look of boredom against a cavern wall as he scanned the area. Despite the fact that that Orrin had taken his primary communicator, he considered using his sparc, a small two way comm hidden within his left ear, but decided against it. Even if he called Dee in to help, there was little chance they would be able to fight passed all of the soldiers and reach the surface.

"Orrin, get everyone to the ships immediately." Von sprinted over, his face red as he barked orders to a few others.

"What has happened?" Orrin hurried over to Von.

"My father is dead. Cole has discovered our location and sent one of his assassin's after us," Von replied.

"What about us?" Rachael stood.

"I have more important things to worry about than you." Von turned to face Rachael. "You are free to go Princess, and I suggest you go quickly."

"Consider us gone." Korso jumped to his feet just as a loud crash shook the cavern. Not waiting for an explanation, he grabbed his weapons and comm off the crate and handed Rachael her sword.

"They're already here?" Von turned, marching towards the rest of his people. "Get everyone to the ships, now!"

"Yes, my Prin… my King." Orrin turned and ran down to a group of soldiers.

"Wait." Rachael started after Von, but Korso grabbed her arm. "You don't have to fight alone. We can help you."

"Forget it Princess. They're gone and so are we." Korso pulled her back towards the tunnel they had taken from the surface.

The caverns began to rumble with growing frequency causing clouds of dirt and small bits of rock to shower them with each explosive impact as they sprinted through the winding corridors. Reaching the surface, Korso spotted two assault class frigates floating over the caves, raining down cannon fire. There was a third frigate, painted in the black and gray colors of the EDM, floating above rest.

Racing to the boulders that they landed by, Korso deactivated the hologram around the shuttle and jumped into the pilot's seat, forcing his apprehension to the back of his mind. Thumbing on the comm while Rachael closed the hatch as she climbed in, Korso powered up the shuttle, hopping the frigates weren't paying close enough attention to notice them. "Dee?"

"Korso?" Dee's voice responded. "I've been trying to reach you. Chaple is here."

"I noticed." Korso pushed on the controls, speeding off the ground.

"How could he have found us this fast?" Rachael asked.

"I don't think he's here for us."

"I have moved the ship to the far side of the planet's moon to avoid detection but it will not take them long to notice," Dee stated.

"Just be ready to bug out the second we get onboard." Korso yanked the controls back, kicking up a large cloud of dust as the shuttle sped off.

"Already am."

Rachael shot a glance at Korso, holding on to her seat. "Can this tub outrun Chaple?"

"Of course." Korso flashed a cocky grin before returning his attention to navigating between the first two ships. "So long as we don't get hit by their plasma cannons."

Rolling the shuttle to the right, and cursing whoever might have been at the targeting computer of the large frigate, Korso shot past Chaple's ship. Bucking from both cannon fire and the planet's atmosphere, he banked right, accelerating towards the *Sprinthawk.*

Korso veered the shuttle around the planets moon, and back into the *Sprinthawk* with a heavy sense of tension hanging over him, one he never managed to get used to despite his years of combat. Vaulting out of the shuttle as it rose into the cargo hold, he dashed up to the cockpit, sliding into the co-pilots seat while Dee pulled the ship away from the moon.

"You seem to have a knack for attracting trouble." Dee winced, jerking the controls to the left an instant before a flash of orange energy flew by.

"Remind me to work on that." Bringing up the nav-computer, Korso began inputting coordinates, trying to ignore the bucking of the ship from every impact on the shields. Spotting Rachael stumble her way in, Korso turned briefly, pointing to the terminal behind the pilot's seat. "Think you can handle the weapons console, Princess?"

"Think you can handle getting us the hell out of here?" Rachael retorted taking the weapons controls. "And we're being followed. IFF reads as the *Black Bell.*"

"It's Chaple," Dee exclaimed, rolling the ship to avoid another barrage of plasma fire.

"I thought you said this tub was fast?" Rachael began firing the aft turrets. "Faster would be better about now."

"Ya think?" Korso snapped, sliding the lever that activated the fold-generator. An electronic hum, rising from the engine room, began to resonate throughout the ship, when another barrage of cannon fire rocked the ship. The hum shifted to an electronic crackling with a sporadic whine, as the ship began to buck and shake enough for him to feel the vibrations through his teeth. "Ooh, that can't be good."

"What? What can't be good?" Rachael twisted towards him, but before he could answer, the hull began to glow. An instant later, the ship zipped off, tearing through what looked like a cloud of azure dust.

* * *

Monitors flashed as various images and lines of text scrolled across the screens covering the mat black walls, gave the information center aboard the imperial transport an odd sense of isolation, despite being able to reach the near entirety of the known galaxy. Ignoring the handfull of techs trying hard to keep themselves occupied throughout the room, Cole stood over one of the central workstations, keeping his scrutinizing gaze on the images floating over the large computer.

The sound of a man moving with a purpose drew Cole's attention away from the holographic image being projected next to him, and towards the man clad in the blue and red uniform of the Ethrian army.

"Lord Cole, Chaple has just sent word that he has driven the T'loak Prince off the planet." The soldier bowed.

"Good," Cole replied.

"He also reports that the Princess was on the planet as well."

Cole raised a curious eyebrow. "Is she dead?"

"Her ship folded before he could capture her, sir. Should I tell him to begin pursuit?"

"No, that won't be necessary. I've already dispatched someone else to handle that task. Tell Chaple to focus on finding the bastard T'loak Prince and bring me his head."

"As you wish sire."

Waiting for the soldier to leave, Cole turned towards the image of the middle-aged man standing next him. "Captain Vega."

"Yes sir."

"You have your orders. If possible, bring Princess Rachael and Korso back alive. I think a public execution of two odious traitors would be a most fitting follow up to my official coronation."

"This is a great deal of talent to waste on two people. I hardly feel it necessary to send my entire platoon," Vega stated, his voice thick with the gruff accent typical of people from the planet Gaelle.

"Was I in anyway unclear, Captain?" Annoyed, Cole let a contemptuous look wash over his face. "Rest assured, that despite his flippant nature, Korso is no fool. He is well trained, highly skilled, and driven by the greatest motivator of all, survival. You will need all of your men and every resource available to you in order capture Korso." He paused, letting his warning penetrate the Captain's graying skull. "And if you should feel the need to question my orders again, by the time you finish your last syllable, there won't be enough left of your corpse to fill a bottle of ale. Understand?"

"Perfectly sir." Vega straightened, swallowing visibly, even with the usual distortion of holo-communications. "I apologize if I spoke out of turn."

"Report success Captain, and all is forgiven." Not bothering to acknowledge Vega's bow, Cole cut off the transmission and returned his attention to the images in front of him.

CHAPTER FOUR

Korso made his way up to the cockpit, flipping an eight inch lavender crystal between his fingers, with a single question running through his mind. It was a question he tried to find the answer to every time he replayed the events in the palace halls. *Why*?

Stepping through the open hatch of the cockpit, Korso found Dee and Rachael standing over the communications terminal, looking at a three dimensional holographic star chart. "What's this?"

"We figured out where we are," Rachael answered, pointing at a familiar green planet. "Here's Ethria, and here we are, way, way down here."

"Did you find out what was wrong with the fold system?" Dee asked.

"Yep." Korso tossed the charred crystal at Dee. "Regulator crystal is totally fried."

Dee shook his head, setting the crystal aside with a sigh. "Did I not tell you that we should have gotten another?"

"You said it would last for at least another month."

"That was a month ago." Dee rolled his eyes.

"Yeah, yeah, the point is we need another one or it's gonna be a *long* trip home." Korso turned the pilot's seat towards the chart and flopped down.

"So we pick one up from a nearby planet." Rachael began cycling through a list of planets, stopping on a small red world. "We're close to the Landara system. I'm sure we can get another on Ruetain."

"Great idea, Princess." Korso leaned back, waving his hands. "Let's just fly over to the planet of paranoid feather heads and hope they don't gouge our eyes out before they turn us over to Cole."

"The Ruetish are outside of Ethrian space, and have no ties to Cole." Rachael turned towards Korso, her emerald eyes shimmering despite her glare. "There's no reason we can't go there."

"They have no *official* ties, but they're as opportunistic as the vacuum is cold."

"I believe Korso is correct," Dee stated. "The Ruetish are not the most welcoming to off-worlders."

"So you have a better idea?" Rachael raised a questioning eyebrow.

Korso held her fiery gaze as he jabbed his thumb to the side. "You can always get out and push."

"What did you have in mind?" Dee asked, cutting off whatever retort Rachael was about to start.

Shooting to his feet, Korso stepped over to the chart and cycled through a few more planets, stopping at a familiar name in the Talnema system. "We go to Secundus. It'll take a week or so to get there on sub-lights alone, but it's far enough from Ethrian space, just within our fuel range, and we can get any anything we need."

"I've never heard of the planet." Rachael shrugged.

Dee moved over to the helm and began inputting the coordinates. "It's a commerce planet, one not really under the control of any galactic power. But there are closer planets."

"Yeah," Korso acknowledged, turning to leave. "But there's something I need to find on Secundus."

"Ah," Dee replied.

"What something?" Rachael asked, following behind him.

Still focusing on the question swimming through his mind, Korso headed down to the galley. Stepping behind a tanned counter, he turned to face Rachael. "You might not realize this, but I'm not much for getting questioned on my own ship."

"You do realize that since my father is gone, you answer to me now." Rachael matched his glare, the light from the overhead glow-rods accentuating her fiery red hair.

"Technically, until you're *officially* crowned Empress, I'm still in charge."

"That technicality only matters in times of war, which we're not in at the moment."

"Then it's a good thing we're on my ship!" Korso slid open a drawer to his right and pulled out two ration bars. Setting one down in front of him, he ripped the brown wrapper off the other and took a bite.

"Just tell me what's on Secundus."

"Besides being a perfect place to hide and get the parts we need, Cole has a safe house in one of the smaller cities. I'm gonna sneak in and see if I can't figure out why he's doing all of this."

"He's a power crazed murderer," Rachael scoffed. "Who cares why he did it."

"I care," Korso snapped. "I know Cole. He's always been ambitious, but there was always a logical reason behind everything he did. He wouldn't go through all the trouble to frame you and me, attack the T'loak, and kill your father simply to grab power. He's a strategist. With Cole, there's always an end game, and if we want to survive, clear our names, and get our lives back, we have to figure out what he's trying to achieve."

Rachael sat on one of the chrome stools opposite him, her fierce green eyes softening. "Dee told me you and Cole had a history. He said you fought in the war together."

"We grew up together." Korso leaned on the counter, letting his anger fade as he bit into the bar again. "Growing up, we were the only friends we had. Partners in danger and all things suicidal, even as kids."

Rachael looked down at the polished counter top for a long minute, considering something, before breaking the silence. "I never thanked you for helping me, or saving my life."

"And you don't have to." Korso slid the second bar over towards her. "Hungry?"

"Yeah." Rachael tore open the wrapper and bit into the cream colored bar, only to make a slight gaging noise as she dropped the bar and spit into her hand. "What the zhod is that? That's the most vile piece of dren I've ever tasted."

"Military ration bars, packed with all the vitamins, nutrients, and proteins a soldier needs to stay healthy, able, and alive on the field." Korso smirked, biting into the bar again. "And no, you don't get use to the taste."

"First thing I do when I become Empress is find a way to improve these." Rachael shoved the bar back to Korso.

"I'll hold you to that Princess."

* * *

Farina, a small, sparsely populated world at the edge of T'loak space, still bore the scars from the war waged by the Ethrians and Hestrons years ago. A war the T'loak had participated in simply because of an ancestral alliance with Hestra and a rivalry with Ethria that few remembered the cause for. A charred husk compared to its former elegance, Farina had been abandoned after the death of the Hestron warlord Raj, with most of the population relocating to other worlds.

Glaring down at a camp of Ethrian soldiers from atop a charred hill of rubble and dirt outside the ruined city of Adom, Von slid a rectangular plasma pack into a mat black pulse rifle, when he noticed the sound of someone approaching.

"What do you want Orrin?" Von peered over his shoulder.

"Majesty, I cannot let you head off on your own in the dead of night," Orrin replied. "Let me gather the others, and then we can all attack together."

"I'm going alone." Von turned to face the troubled man. Orrin had been at his side for years, always acting as the voice of reason. He was a loyal friend, even when Von's temper got the better of him, and he was one of the few Von listened to. But not today. Today he needed to be strong, to be cruel and rash. He had a duty. His enemies were laughing, enjoying a warm starry night around a fire while his people suffered. "This is my fight, and I won't lead you to your grave."

"I realize that you want to avenge your father's death, but you are King now, and you must think of all those whom you hold dominion over."

"My people are being persecuted! Our homeworld is in ruins, and we are the targets of assignation. As the last heir to the T'loak throne, it is my duty to kill all who oppose me." Von pushed past Orrin. "Cole dies by my hand."

"Lord Von, alone you cannot defeat Cole and his armies." Orrin followed after him. "If you really want to defeat Cole then we should seek allies who hate him as much as you."

"Who?" Von spun on his heel, letting his anger boil over and twist his face. "There is no one else that would oppose the Emperor of Ethria."

"Princess Rachael is the rightful ruler. Reports from Ethria indicate that there are still soldiers who would follow her, and she travels with the Seraph Prime. Allied together, you could raise an army that could defeat Cole before he consolidates his power."

"And how would I find her? She fled Slovac days ago. She could be anywhere in the galaxy."

"Give me time, and I will bring her to you."

Von let his anger subside for a moment, considering Orrin's words. "Very well."

"Then you'll hold off on your attack?" Orrin asked.

"I will hold off attacking Cole until you return." Von nodded. "But those in the camp will still suffer the wrath of the T'loak."

"Lord Von…"

“I will not argue with you any further.” Von turned and started down the hill. “Go and find the Princess. I’ll wait for you in the Temple of Raj.”

Stopping halfway down the dark hill to wait for Orrin to leave, Von made his way down to a large boulder near the outskirts of the camp. Eight soldiers, sitting around a campfire drinking and laughing, caught Von’s attention as he took in the layout of the camp. Sneaking around one of the sand colored tents, he found two more soldiers talking, and another walking along the perimeter.

Grateful for the lack of moonlight, Von sneaked over to where the soldier was patrolling and drove the butt of his rifle to back of the soldier’s head. Before the soldier could cry out for help, Von rammed his rifle into his temple. Taking a grenade off the prone man’s belt, he scurried back to the two soldiers talking and hid in the shadow of a dead tree.

Taking a calming breath, Von twisted the top of the cone shaped grenade, switching the setting from safe to armed, and threw the grenade over the heads of the talking soldiers and watched as it landed in front of the men sitting by the fire. The grenade exploded, cutting off any thoughts the soldiers might have had about running with burst of green flame.

“What the hell was that?” The two soldiers closest to Von turned to see what had happened, but before they could get an answer, Von jumped to his feet, killing both with a burst of shots to the chest.

Stepping passed the men he had shot, Von went over to fire, checking the bodies of the soldiers caught in the explosion with a kick. Finding two survivors, both severely burned and bleeding from shrapnel, he shot them both in the heart. Certain that all of the soldiers were dead, Von turned to examine the tents when he spotted a man in dark blue charging towards him.

Von took quick aim and loosed a stream of auburn rounds flying towards the man, a Captain, based on the insignia on his chest.

Darting to the left to avoid getting torn to shreds by the plasma rounds, the Captain slammed his shoulder into Von's chest, knocking him down. Von rolled to his feet with a growl, leveling his rifle to fire again, only to have it batted out of his hands by the Captains unfolding sword. The Captain continued his attacks, intent on ending their bout with a single blow, and forced Von to jump backwards. Yanking his own weapon off his belt, Von thumbed the release on the silver handle, causing it to extend to a six foot spear.

Parrying an overhead strike, Von hit the Captain with a jab to the ribs. Von, just as egger to finish off his opponent, swung for his head, but the Captain managed raise his sword, blocking his strike. Taking advantage of the opening, the Captain unleashed a flurry of attacks, forcing Von on the defensive. Attempting to dodge a horizontal slash, a pained grunt slipped through his lips as the cold tip of the Captain's sword caught his side. The Captain swung again, but Von rolled to right, twisting as he rose and sent his spear flying into the back of the Captain's knee.

The Captain dropped to one knee, crying out in pain, while Von spun and struck him across the face. Anger pulsing through him with every beat of his heart, Von dropped his spear and ripped the sword from the Captain's hand before holding the tip a few centimeters above his right eye.

"Please… don't."

"I will kill all of my enemies." Von drove the sword through the top of the Captain's shoulder, and down into his heart. Leaving the sword sticking out of the Captain's torso as he picked up his spear and retracted it, Von forced himself to take a few breaths, trying to slow the torrent of rage and adrenaline that kept his hands shaking. Tearing a piece of cloth free from one of the tents to use as a bandage for his side, he began searching the tents, wondering how many Ethrians he would have to kill before the void his father's death had created would begin to close.

* * *

"So, was there a plan to get inside, or…" Rachael trialed off, glaring at the side of Korso's head.

Replying with a sneer, Korso glanced down the sparse roadway towards the single story complex that served as an EDM safe house. The building was unremarkable in appearance, its cream colored walls and tinted windows blending in with the other structures lining the street. Anyone passing by would have glanced at the sign and assumed it was another office building, unless they were familiar with Ethrian military code, and Cole's sense of humor.

"It appears the building is fairly empty." Dee turned towards Korso. "But how *do* you plan to get in?"

"Through the front door," Korso replied in a flat tone, but a raised eyebrow from his companions compelled him to elaborate. "This place is pretty far out from Ethrian space and it's been kept off the grid, right? So with everything that's going on, I doubt Cole has had time to comm in our supposed traitor status. And it's even more unlikely he's had time to change *all* of the military access codes, especially the older ones. So we walk up to the front door, punch in the code to open it up, and stroll in."

"And if we're recognized by whatever security Cole has in there?" Rachael asked.

"We get spotted, we run." Korso shrugged.

"That's your plan?" Rachael turned towards Korso, jabbing him with a finger. "*Run*? That's a stupid plan. Running's not even a plan. Running's what you do when a plan fails."

"And I suppose her royal painness has a better idea?"

Rachael glanced to the side, crossing her arms with a scowl. "Um… well… no, but then it wasn't my idea to come here in the first place. I suggested hiding."

"How is hide better than run?" Korso matched her gaze, trying to suppress a smirk. "And, actually I had another idea but I figured it was a touch of overkill."

"That being?"

"We storm the place and take what we need."

"I am not going to attack one of our own safe houses and hurt loyal Ethrians, even if Cole is secretly running the place."

"It's plan A or plan B."

Rolling her eyes with an annoyed sigh, Rachael turned back towards the building. "Plan A."

Smiling at some unsaid joke, Dee gestured towards the end of the avenue. "If you two have finished, perhaps we can move this along. Unless you need a moment or two, I'd understand."

"Is he mocking us?" Rachael pushed passed the taller man and started towards their target.

"You know, I think he is." Korso followed alongside Dee, shaking his head in mock disgust. "Stop that."

Reaching the buildings entrance, Korso stepped over to the access pad and keyed in an older code issued to all top ranking officers, including Cole. Waiting for the soft beep that signified the unlocking of the doors an instant before they slid apart, Korso stepped into a cool reception hall, his right hand instinctively moving to his pistol as he scanned the room, half expecting an alarm to go off at any second. A crescent shaped desk sat in the center of the tiled lobby while a few colorful plants from different worlds sat in blue and gold pots scattered around the room, and an intricate marble fountain splashed water in the far corner.

Catching a nod from Dee, Korso crept past the desk, picking up the sound of voices as he entered a short unlit hall. Mindful of each step as his boots touched the verdant tiled floor, he spotted a blond haired woman in brown, no doubt an employee, arguing with a man in an EDM uniform in a small waiting room.

"I told your boss already that I've done everything I can to speed up your departure time, but port security still has the final say when any potentially hazardous material passes through here." The woman started past a small triangular table sitting between matching couches, but the soldier grabbed her by the arm and spun her around.

"And I told you that's not good enough. We have a shipment that needs delivering and…" the soldier trailed off, turning towards Korso and the others as they stepped out of the hall. "You? You're not supposed to be here."

"No, it's okay. I have clearance." Korso put on a warm smile and held his hands up as he approached the confused looking soldier.

"What?" the soldier replied, tilting his head.

Korso let his smile broaden as he closed the distance between himself and the soldier before driving his fist into the unsuspecting man's stomach. Nailing him with a knee to the face as he doubled over gasping for air, Korso punched him across the jaw and watched as he fell back onto a couch, unconscious.

"Was that necessary?" Rachael glanced at Korso with an annoyed scowl on her face.

"I could have shot him." Korso shrugged before turning towards the blond woman. "So how are you?"

"Um… not that I didn't enjoy seeing that jerk getting punched out, but aren't you with him?" the woman asked, glancing at each of them. "You guys are military right? Won't you get in trouble?"

Korso shook his head with an amused grin. "We're with a different department, and I out rank him. Besides, I really don't like those EDM guys."

"Tell me about it," the woman scoffed. "Those jerks have been hounding me all day."

Korso flashed a warm smile. "They have a knack for that; and I don't think I caught your name."

"Priscilla Louis, but you can call me Pris."

"Pris it is then." Korso nodded, shaking her hand.

"So what can I do for you?" Pris asked, moving a lock of her curly hair from her eyes.

"Actually Priscilla, there was a mix up with some files we needed," Rachael stated, stepping between Pris and Korso. "If you could help us with that, we'll get out of your way. *Right Captain*?"

"Right, the files," Korso agreed, noting with painful clarity that Rachael's heel had found his foot. "Someone forgot to dot some I's and checked the wrong box on a form and our files got lost in the void of the net. So rather than start the requisition process over again, I figured I'd just stop in pick up the files from the computer myself."

Pris gave an understanding nod. "I'd love to help, but all the files within the computers are for authorized personnel only and there's no one here who can request clearance for you. You came right in-between work cycles."

"You're the only one here?" Dee looked towards Pris.

"In-between cycles there are usually two people on call, but those EDM jerks dragged my friend off when they got here; said they needed her for some reason," Pris explained.

"It's fine," Korso stated. "I have Cole's access code. I just need you to point me at his computer."

"Oh, no problem. It's right down here." Pris smiled, stepping towards a wide hall across the room before looking back to Korso. "This is going to sound weird but you look kinda familiar."

"Really? Can't imagine why." Korso shrugged, hopping that she wouldn't figure out who they actually were.

"Why is the EDM here on Secundus?" Dee asked while Pris led them passed the empty offices of the other employees.

"Not sure. They arrived late last night and dragged my friend off early this morning before demanding I get them cleared to leave." Pris paused at a large oval shaped door and pushed it open. "Here we are."

"Thanks." Korso stepped into the large office just as the overhead lights blinked on and suppressed a laugh, noticing the ancient painting hanging on the paneled walls. Unsurprised by the obsessive organization of Cole's shelves and bookcases, he dropped down into an expensive chair behind the curved graywood desk with exaggerated exhaustion. "Even way out here, he decorates the place with that pre-exodus art crap."

Dee shook his head, standing next to Korso as he flipped a switch and raised the monitor from its compartment within the desk. "Some would argue that preserving artifacts from the original homeworld is a worthy endeavor."

"And I say that it's a wasted effort to cling to a world that's long since dead." Korso scoffed. "Been over a thousand years since the exodus, Earth's a figment no one remembers."

"At least he has taste." Rachael paused by a painting of a general on horseback. "These have to be worth a fortune, how did Cole get ahold of them?"

"Spoils of war. But knowing him, those are probably just copies. His *refined palate* would never allow him to let the real ones get too far from him." Accessing Cole's files with his own codes, Korso scanned over the names of various files, glad to see that some of his older classified codes still worked. *It would be far too convenient to just label one: treasonous plan to betray the Empire.*

After twenty minutes of searching, he began to wonder if he was wasting his time when a file name caught his attention. Opening the folder, his sense of confusion began to swell as he read the pages on the monitor and clicked over to a linked file.

"Find anything?" Rachael asked, sitting in the chair across from him while Dee kept Pris distracted.

"I'm not sure." Korso shrugged. "There's some notes about a treaty, but I have no clue what it's about. Plus, I found some fragmented files buried within a file from the Galactic Affairs Ministry about a coalition of worlds."

"He's probably talking about the treaty you and Dee oversaw," Rachael stated, stepping over to lean over his shoulder.

Korso shook his head, surprised by the pleasant fragrance filling his nostrils as she leaned closer. "Timing's wrong."

"Then what? The GAM handles all treaties, not the EDM. The only reason you were involved with the Hestron treaty was because my dad asked." Rachael scrolled across the screen and opened another file.

"I know," Korso retorted. "But Cole's involved with this one somehow, and your father knew about it. I found a few messages of them arguing about how to handle it. What I don't get is why. The war with the Hestrons was over, and with it, any active aggression between the T'loak and us. So why would your father or the GAM or Cole care about any other treaty? And who was it with, and why wasn't I briefed on it? I can't find any mention about who's even in this coalition."

"I wonder if this is what my dad and that bastard were arguing about in the throne room."

"Maybe, but even if it is, none of this explains why Cole seized power," Korso growled, resisting the urge to shoot the monitor.

"We're obviously missing something. Cole goes from griping about this coalition to wanting to attack the T'loak. Whatever happened in-between is what got my father killed." Rachael looked towards him, anger giving her green eyes a vibrant flare. "Some of these files are sub-linked through the GAM. Can't you access them?"

"Not without broadcasting to every security system in Ethrian space our location. I'm already gambling that some of the code's I used aren't flagged yet." The sound of someone approaching caused Korso to peer out the door just as Dee walked in. "How's our hostess?"

"Distracted." Dee waved a genpad before punching the keys at the bottom. "I found this on her desk. It's a shipping manifest.

Most of it mundane: food stuffs, water, meds, but one item was added last minute and ordered for express delivery specifically by Cole."

"What is it?" Rachael asked, standing upright.

Dee shook his head. "The order was vague, referred to only as the package, and listed as alpha-oh-one."

"Meaning?" Rachael waved a hand for Dee to continue.

"Its military code, highest priority to be delivered at all costs," Korso replied.

Rachael arched an eyebrow. "So it's important to Cole?"

"And explains why the EDM are here." Dee nodded.

"Yep." Korso allowed a smirk to replace his frustrated scowl, relishing the thought of irritating Cole. "Let's go steal it."

CHAPTER FIVE

The faint but familiar sounds of planetary entry reverberated off the angular hull of the *Crimson Sword*, a large frigate-class warship, as it neared Secundus. Standing on the hilt of the painted logo etched into the metallic floor plates of the command information center, a man whose hair had just began to gray watched in silence as the first of many planetary cities became visible through the tinted viewport in front of him.

"Captain Vega, we just received a coded message from command." Lira, a tall, short haired woman in her thirties, stood near the comm station.

"Go ahead Lieutenant," Vega replied, letting his dry, gruff voice carry over the constant stream of noise as the crew carried out their duties.

"We have a probable location on the target: Ordan, near the local port."

"Very Good." Vega turned and marched towards the lift at the rear of the CIC. "Have Lieutenant Tyler meet me in the transport room with beta squad."

"Understood sir."

* * *

"I really don't think this is a good idea," Rachael stated from Korso's left as they emerged from a private passageway that linked the safe house to the Ordan City Port.

"Sure it is." Korso hurried through the crowded, climate controlled corridors, filtering out the storm of a thousand different beings trying to talk over each other and kept one eye on the genpad Dee held.

"So long as we remain a step behind Cole, we'll never be able to remove him from the throne." Dee turned, leading them up a flight of stairs before heading down another wide and brightly lit walkway. "This is our best chance to get ahead of him."

Korso took the pad from Dee, showing it to Rachael while pointing to a portion of the port terminal on the display screen. "According to the info we conned out of Pris, Cole's slack jawed igits got stalled by customs, right? And their ship is here, in a private dock. So all we gotta do is cut them off, take the package, and bolt before they get there. Easy-peasy."

Rachael veered around an overweight Hespen with a doubtful look on her face. "Walking up to a ship full of EDM goons to steal their super-secret mystery box isn't what I'd traditionally call easy."

"Sadly that's more a testament to how my life goes than an annoyingly sarcastic comment…" Korso trailed off, spotting the sealed door they were looking for and typed in the access code Pris had provided once they reached it. "Besides, we're not going to their ship. We're gonna hit them before they get there."

"And what about the port security, which are only doing their jobs, are you going to *hit* them too?" Rachael glanced at Korso.

"I'm not Cole." Korso let some of his anger lace his tone. "I'll be aiming to incapacitate not kill. But considering that they won't be returning that sentiment, you need to realize it's us or them."

"There's a plaza ahead that's sealed from most public traffic that should suit our purpose." Dee gestured towards a descending ramp as the door hissed closed behind them.

Following Dee down the ramp, Korso looked over the plaza, noting the positions of large potted plants from unknown worlds and marble benches scattered about the quiet area. Taking one last look at the genpad to verify their position and make sure he knew which way to run should things go south, he tossed the device into a thick burgundy bush before ducking behind a curved bench.

Slipping behind a triangular pillar, Dee slipped his pistol out of its holster, checking the charge as he did. "We'll need to be quick.

I doubt port security will give us much time after the first shots are fired."

"Fast it is then." Korso readied one of his own pistols.

"You know, if you're going to keep dragging me into trouble like this, then you should probably give me a pulse pistol too," Rachael whispered, crouching next at Korso's side.

"Can you even us one?" Korso shot the Princess a skeptical look.

"Better than you, I bet." Rachael leaned toward him, narrowing her eyes.

Suppressing a smirk and a pang of annoyance, he started to reply when a door thirty yards ahead hissed open. Peering around the bench as the door slid closed, Korso spotted half a dozen of Cole's men walking a large black crate on a hovering cart.

Korso leaned out, picking his target, and fired. Following his lead, Dee fired an instant behind, catching two of the soldiers on the chest.

"Cover," a soldier shouted, ducking for cover, only to get twisted sideways as Korso shot him in the shoulder and chest.

The remaining two, each behind sufficient cover, began to return fire. *Glad they used thick marble in this place.* Korso ducked back behind the bench as a volley of plasma rounds peppered the bench. Letting the familiar sense of tension wash over him, he rolled behind a thick column with a boisterous shout and fired a dozen rounds at the soldiers, not caring much if he hit them. He grinned, letting a barrage of angry shouts and enemy fire force him back behind the column. *That got their attention. Idiots.*

Distracted by the obnoxious man who had just unloaded on them, the soldiers concentrated their fire on Korso. A mistake realized too late when Dee darted towards them from their blind side and fired with practiced aim, killing them both.

"I am always amazed at how often that works," Dee stated with a smirk, stepping over to the crate.

"I know, right." Korso glanced around, conscious of the fact that they had a minute or two before reinforcements arrived. "So what do we have?"

Punching a few keys on the pad built into the crates LED, Dee gazed over the small screen for a moment before letting out a displeased growl.

"Well?" Korso turned towards Dee.

"Nothing good." Dee looked over his shoulder. "Thermal grenades, a pair of rochling shells, and… I'm not certain but this looks like the chemical components for an HVBB."

"What's that, besides bad?" Rachael asked.

"High Velocity Bunker Buster, but that doesn't make any sense." His mind swimming in disbelief, Korso darted towards the crate to see for himself. "Cole wouldn't use any of this. He always said it was a waste of enemy resources. There's got to be more."

Dee shook his head. "There isn't."

"Then we missed something!"

"We didn't."

"Guys," Rachael called, staring through a porthole while locking the door the soldiers had entered. "Port security is coming and they look angry."

"Then let's not be here to greet them," Dee stated.

This doesn't track. Why would he need this, and what does he want dead so bad he'd go to this extreme? Ignoring the sound of Rachael running passed him, Korso slammed his fist on the screen with a growl.

Dee grabbed his arm, spinning him away from the crate. "Korso, we need to go."

"There's something we're missing."

"Perhaps, but we won't find it today." Dee pulled him towards one of the doors behind them.

Noticing the sound of the security guards forcing the door open, Korso cursed, unwilling to give up his only chance for a lead, but realized he had little choice. Nodding, he hurried after Rachael as she reached an oval door across from the crate.

Rachael quickly pressed the switch that opened the heavy metal door to what was supposed to be an empty catwalk, and muttered a curse of her own as she backed into Korso.

"Princess, how nice of you to make finding you so easy." A middle aged man in crimson body armor, flanked by a dozen similarly dressed soldiers, flashed a cold smile.

Glancing over his shoulder, Korso spotted a five man team of security guards break through the door and take up positions behind them. Trying to suppress a growing sense of dread, he looked back to the man and smiled. "So you must be the latest monkey Cole decided to throw on my back."

"I'm Pytor Vega, Captain of the Crimson Knights."

"Oh, I hear you guys are good." Korso kept his eyes on Vega, but noticed Rachael's left hand moving up his thigh, before resting on his pistol.

"The best." Vega straightened, pride pouring from every word. "You are caught, surrounded, and beaten. Surrender now and I promise you'll live to see a trail."

"Or…" Rachael kicked Vega in the face, knocking him backwards, while drawing one of Korso's pistols, shooting a knight with her left hand, and slapped the switch that closed the door.

Yanking his second pistol free while she shot the door control panel, Korso spun around firing a volley at the soldiers behind them before they could react. Ducking behind cover, the soldiers began to return fire, but Rachael deftly shot the light fixtures hanging above, dropping the florescent lights on top of them.

"Not bad, Princess." Korso smirked, running behind Dee towards the door they had used to enter the plaza.

"Not bad? I was brilliant," Rachael stated, keeping pace with Korso. "Now how do you intend to get us out of here?"

Korso smirked. "Plan B, we run."

"Still not a plan." Rachael rolled her eyes.

Sprinting back into the main terminal, Korso winced at the sounds of panicked beings as the intercom requested them to remain calm while security apprehended dangerous criminals—as if calm remained an option. The port security was well trained and thorough, sealing off doorways and positioning guards in every conceivable path they could, but they were also sloppy. There was a reason swords and knives were still in fashion despite all the advances humans have made in weaponry. A missed shot from a firearm, or even a perfect one, would send a plasma round burning through two or three people, and security was firing a lot of rounds.

Navigating through the crowd and corridors as fast as he could, Korso fired at the pursuing knights and security, careful to avoid clusters of panicked civilians. Ahead, he saw a squad of guard's fire at Rachael—prompting her to roll behind a tan pillar—before turning to fire on Korso and Dee, forcing them slide behind a large fountain.

Leaving Dee and Rachael to occupy the guards ahead of them, Korso pulled a chrome disk from a pocket, arming it as he turned back towards the way they had come, and flung it at their pursuers an instant before it exploded in an intense flash of blinding light.

"It won't take them long pin us down," Dee shouted between exchanges of plasma rounds.

"I noticed." Korso swiftly dispatched the wave of knights behind them before glancing around. Recognizing their location from the port map, he smiled and motioned towards a large tinted window a few feet away from Rachael. "Luckily our exit is at hand."

Still firing at the guards ahead, Dee peaked at the window and nodded. "Vega has to be watching the docks. He'll know if we take a transport."

"I'm counting on it. He expects us to go up, so we go down. We use the service tunnels to get us back into the city." Pulling another flash bang from his pocket, Korso looked towards Rachael. "Get ready to move."

Waiting for her acknowledgement, Korso threw the flash bang at their attackers before shooting the window. Adrenalin surging, he darted over to the shattered window and jumped, rolling through the ten foot drop to a hanger floor a moment before Dee and Rachael.

"Won't they catch us if we take a ship?" Rachael asked from behind as they ducked into the shadow of a large freighter.

"Indeed." Dee nodded.

Rachael spun towards Korso, wearing a confused look. "Then why…"

"Relax Princess; it's all part of the plan." Korso grinned, spotting the access shaft to the service tunnels. "Dee, feed them the rabbit."

Dee smirked, pulling a small digital device from his belt. "Already done."

* * *

"Report." Vega marched into the port control room, unimpressed by the security's efforts to apprehend the Princess and her cohorts.

"Sir, security reports losing the target in hanger one two niner," Lieutenant Tyler answered, turning to face him with stiff shoulders and his hands clasped behind his back.

Vega laughed, shaking his head in disappointment. Korso was supposed to be some brilliant military genius, but the ease in tracking the man was laughable. "No doubt running to his ship. Order the *Sword* to scan for the *Sprinthawk's* IDC."

"Yes sir." Tyler turned towards the console to his left and relayed the order. Waiting with his hands behind his back, Vega glanced over to the wall of monitors opposite the entrance, pleased to see his men taking control of the chaos in the terminal.

"Lira has them on scanners," Tyler stated.

"Tell her to fire when ready."

"Weapon's—what?" Tyler turned back to the console, pressing his headset against his ear. "Say again… How, you just had them?"

"Lieutenant?" Vega shot a glare at Tyler, not liking the tone in his voice.

"Sir, the ship detected the *Sprinthawk's* registered ident-code, but it was rigged to a long-range probe. There's no sign of the *Sprinthawk*." Tyler straightened. "Given that the port wasn't completely locked down yet, they may have escaped using a modified IDC, or…"

"So they're gone?"

"Yes sir."

Vega swallowed—biting back a wave of anger and humiliation—and took a long breath. "Order the ship to begin scanning for any sign of the *Sprinthawk* or any anomalous signal. Then take your squad and tear this place apart. The Princess may still be close by."

"Yes sir."

Well played, Vega mused. At least now he understood why Korso was so highly regarded. Underestimating his opponent had been a mistake, but it was one that would not be repeated. Cole had ordered him to capture Korso and the Princess, and he intended to see that order executed with surgical precision.

* * *

Orrin stood behind a young man on the bridge of a small carrier ship approaching the edge of the Talnema system, and looked down at a monitor displaying a holographic map. "What is it you wanted to see me about?"

"We just intercepted a message from the Crimson Knights saying that the Princess has escaped and may be heading back out to space."

"Any ships on the scanners?"

"None."

"So she's still on the planet." Orrin crossed his arms wondering what might be happening. "And they have no idea where she is now?"

"No sir, but if they're still on-world we might be able to track them."

"Good, we have to find them before the Crimson Knights do." Orrin clapped the man on the shoulder as he turned to leave. As he walked down the narrow corridor, he began to ponder how he would convince the Princess to join forces with King Von, but he decided to figure that out once he managed found her.

* * *

Korso sat in the pilots chair of the *Sprinthawk*—having decided to move the ship to a different port after the previous days jaunt through Ordan—and finished shutting down the primary systems. Peering through the forward viewport, he noticed the sun had just begun to set over the large city of Durakeen.

Satisfied that the computers were locked down from any possible hacking attempts the sleazy dock manager might try, he made his way to a small locker near the back of the bridge, sliding it open as he reached it, and pulled out a pulse pistol and holster before extending his hand towards Rachael.

Rachael tilted her head, blinking in confusion before taking the weapon. "What's this?"

"It's a pistol. You asked for it, remember?" Korso leaned back against a bulkhead. "You're not quite as horrible a shot as I thought. But if you'd rather not have it…"

Dee stepped passed Korso and reached for his preferred weapon, a four foot long war axe with a thick spike at the handles end, and retracted it to the size of a hatchet before tucking it into his belt. "For him, that's an olive branch. You should take it, they are rare."

With a slight Smile curling her lips, Rachael began looping the holster through her belt and looked back to Korso. "So you think I'll need to use this?"

"You've never been here before have you?" Korso smirked. "Your pacifistic kindhearted attitude will only get that pretty face of yours shot or… defiled, and I'd rather not see that happen." He stepped back to the locker and pulled out a thin half inch long comm, and handed it to Rachael.

"What's this… did you just call me pretty?" Rachael's smile broadened.

"No," Korso retorted, unable to hide a playful grin. "And it's a long range communicator. Slip it in your ear, tap it once, and you've got an emergency comm; just in case we run into any more trouble."

"It might behoove us to gather our supplies before our pursuers can catch up to us." Dee shook his head with a laugh and headed for the airlock.

"Anyone else hungry?" Korso asked as the three of them walked down the corridor.

"I could eat." Dee shrugged.

"How can you think about food when we're running for our lives all over the galaxy?" Rachael glanced over her shoulder.

"Can't run on an empty stomach," Korso replied with a grin, as they stopped in front of the airlock and waited for it to open. "But don't worry, I promise not to sell you for anything less than a grade B meal."

"B?" Rachael spun on her heel with a smirk and shoved Korso into the crowded hanger. "You're such a jerk."

"Brat." Korso turned to face her, exaggerating his stumble. Stepping over to secure the hatch, he kept his gaze on her, surprised to find himself enjoying her unyielding challenges.

"Cachak." Rachael leaned in close.

"Frau niet posh."

"I know what that means!" Eyes flaring with anger and a hint of a smile, Rachael punched him on the shoulder.

"You know, you swear more than most enlisted men I've met." Korso smirked, rubbing his sore shoulder. "And you hit hard for girl."

"Damn right." Rachael stormed after Dee.

* * *

Vega stood alone in the holo-comm room of the *Crimson Sword* as the lights dimmed and an image of the Ethrian throne flickered into existence a few feet in front of him. A moment later, Cole stepped into the emitters range and sat down wearing a dower expression.

"I've been dealing with dissident troops and pretentious statesmen all day, so for your sake Captain, you had best have good news."

"Lord Cole, we tracked the Princess to Secundus, but unfortunately she escaped… for the moment. We are fairly certain that she is still on the planet, but it'll take us some time before we can locate them." Vega stood straight, trying to keep his voice level and calm.

Cole slammed a fist on the arm of the throne. "Does your incompetence know no bounds? I told you not to underestimate Korso. It was fortuitous that he used an access code that I had already flagged and we learned he was there, but it takes time to change them all and that is not a mistake he will make twice."

"He will be found, sir. My men have already begun to search all probable ports and cities."

"What about the package, or did your amateurish Knights allow him to take that as well?"

"No sir, the package was secured and is in route."

"Good."

"My Lord, you have my personal assurances that I will bring the Princess back to Ethria," Vega stated, making sure his tone and manner conveyed his sincerity.

"That would be for the best, Captain. I do have an Empire to save. Fail again, and I'll hang you with your own entrails." Cole leaned back with an eerie, warm smile. "And Captain…"

"Yes sir?" Vega forced himself to swallow, unnerved by the gleam his saw in Cole's holographic eyes.

"Good hunting," Cole stated, his voice low and filled with venom. A instant later, the transmission cut off, leaving Vega with an icy chill in his gut.

CHAPTER SIX

Beings from every planet in the sector filled the boisterous two-story tavern. Music blared on the lower level, giving some of the clientele something to dance to—the swirling, flashing multi-colored lights added a circus like feel to a sea of writhing patrons—while the second floor was reserved for dinning and the staging of competing conversations.

A Saurian waiter, menacing even without the reddish hue from the lights, struggled to carry a tray of food and drinks up the metal stairs. Getting clear of the stairs, he made his was over to a triangular table that overlooked the dance floor.

"Here is your food." The waiter set a plate in front of Korso and the others. "And two gentlemen down stairs have, how shall I say, made an offer for your lady friend."

"Tell the cachak's no tutin way." Rachael shot the waiter an irritated glare.

"Sure, no skin off my hump," the waiter said as he turned and left.

"What is it with this city?" Rachael asked. "We've barely been here twenty minutes and that's the third time that's happened."

"Durakeen is a place you can buy whatever you want if you got enough credits. Anything from the mundane to the obscene, and where every vice has a market, including guns, drugs, and women. It's all… frightfully uncivilized," Korso quipped with a grin.

"He is right Princess, we must all exercise caution while we are here." Dee nodded as he began to eat.

"Then shouldn't we hide in some place that's actually hidden?" Rachael leaned on her elbows. "You don't know of some hidden moon or space station near the outer rim or the uncharted territories?"

Korso shook his head, noting the scent of the stronger beverages that the air scrubbers failed to filter. "There's nothing out there but smugglers and pirates."

Rachael glanced at Dee. "What's the difference?"

"The smugglers aren't organized," Dee replied.

Korso took a long sip of the sweet-smelling beverage in his mug. "Relax, some of the best hiding places are the ones right under your nose."

"You're nuts, you know that right?" Rachael picked up her fork.

"I'm just good at what I do." Korso lifted his cup with a grin.

"Then they must not have taught you how to make a good plan then. Or was running and shooting all you could remember?"

"Well I'm sorry to disappoint you Princess. I've only saved your life a couple times now," Korso retorted, before tearing a piece of meat off the bone on his plate.

Dee held up a hand, interrupting their latest argument. "Is it at all possible for us to eat in peace?"

"It's possible, but not likely to happen." Rachael stuffed a piece of bread into her mouth, glaring at Korso.

"Hey, I can be quiet just as long as she can," Korso stated.

"No you can't." Rachael rolled her eyes.

"Yes I can." Korso quickly finished his meal, allowing himself to be distracted by the pulsing music before glancing back at Rachael. "So let's say you were in charge—"

"Well, I kinda am." Rachael picked up her cup with a shrug.

"—what's your brilliant plan to get our lives back."

"Well, I'd…" Rachael leaned forward to reply, but a perplexed looked fell over her. "We…"

"Not so easy, is it?"

Rachael let out a sigh and leaned back. "Fine, you've made your point."

Dee pushed his plate to the side, swallowing the last bit of glazed meat. "Until a better solution presents itself, we have little choice but to repair the *Sprinthawk* and remain hidden."

Rachael shrugged, turning towards the older man. "So what all do we need to fix the ship?"

"We used a lot of fuel flying with just the sub-light engines, but that will be covered with the port fees," Dee replied. "I'm a little concerned about the shields though. The patch job we used during our last engagement in the war has been pushed further than I intended. We were going to repair it when we got back to Ethria, but our stay was cut short. It should be an easy fix with the right components."

"Plus we need a regulator crystal for the fold-generator, and when the crystal got fried, it short-circuited a few other systems. We should fix it before it blows up," Korso added.

"Okay, so why don't Dee and I go get the components for the shields while you get the stuff for the fold-generator." Rachael flashed a teasing smile. "That should be simple enough for even you to do without screwing up."

"As you command, your most annoying highness." Korso rose to his feet and twirled his hand in a mock bow.

Waiting to see the sour expression on Rachael's face, he turned and headed down the spiral stairs. He ignored the head jarring pulses of the electronic music and began weaving through the swarm of dancers. Spotting the exit to his right, he twisted around a tall woman in a Ruetish dress, only to bump into a man wearing gray and black Ethrian military fatigues.

"Hey, watch your step." The short, toned man spun around, his hand clenched and ready to strike, but froze mid spin, surprise twisting his face. "Commander Korso?"

"Sergeant Webber?" Surprise surging through him as he recognized the man from his former unit, Korso smiled, reaching for his left pistol with a casual shake of his head. "What are you doing here?"

"I'm hiding in exile, same as you, sir." Webber held his hands out with a shrug. "Once General Cole took control of the empire, anyone who didn't pledge loyalty to him was arrested and killed for conspiracy and treason."

"So why are you here?" Korso glanced over the crowd, searching for any hint of an attack.

"My old man used to tell me that no one ever knew him better than the men he served with. After six years of fighting in and flyin' to one hell hole after the other, I'd say I got to know *you* pretty well." Webber lowered his hands, replacing his smile with a grim look. "When Cole told everyone that you and the Princess had killed the Emperor, I knew he was lying."

"What makes you so sure I didn't kill him?"

"One, it might not have been public knowledge but you were off world negotiating the treaty. Two, why kill the Emperor when you already had command of the army as Supreme Commander. And three, anyone that knows you knows you'd never want to rule. It'd be way too dull, and you'd probably shoot the politicians."

"That only happened once, but good answer." Korso lowered his hand with a relieved laugh and motioned towards the exit. "Let's talk outside."

"Now that I've found you, you can lead us against Cole. We can take our home back," Webber said, following behind Korso as he stepped through the large door and into the brisk night air.

"As much as I'd like to kick Cole in the teeth, the two of us aren't much of an army. And what *us*?"

"Cole doesn't control the entire Ethrian army. Just over half follow his orders, the rest have fled Ethria, and a lot of the ones that stayed aren't too happy about his more aggressive policies. I have our unit camped a system over along with Lieutenant Colonel Dee's Emerald Raiders while I went out to pick up supplies."

"Two platoons aren't enough to launch a full scale assault, but it's enough to do some real damage." Korso took a long breath, trying to slow the thoughts racing through his mind and piece together a next move. Pulling out a pocket sized genpad, Korso brought up the coordinates to a small planet and handed it to Webber. "I want you to track down anyone you can who's still loyal to the Princess or me and meet me in the Azulan system."

Webber looked over the genpad before handing it back to Korso with a confused look. "You're not coming with me?"

"I still gotta fix my ship, but I'll meet you there, got it?"

"Yes sir." Webber saluted.

"Technically we're not in the military right now, so you don't need to salute."

"Then you can't reprimand me if I do." Webber flashed a grin before turning jogging down the street.

* * *

Sticky from blood and dirt, Von stood in front of several dead Ethrian soldiers as he replaced the plasma cartridge of his rifle. Ignoring the dusty night wind stinging his nose, he started towards a large gray tent in the center of the camp, but two plasma rounds shot passed his head, prompting him to dive behind a large boulder and fire blindly. Risking a peak around the boulder, he spotted three soldiers moving towards him, each wearing defense ministry uniforms.

"Lay down your weapon and surrender or we will kill you," one soldier yelled.

A fresh wave of fury surging through him, Von retorted with a growl and another string of shots, catching the arrogant Ethrian in the chest. He pivoted, unleashing a second volley that killed another soldier. The last soldier fired a barrage of orange plasma, forcing him back behind cover and a growing cloud of dust. Eyes stinging,

Von rolled to the other side of the boulder and fired, burning a hole through his foes thigh. Von jumped to his feet, sprinting towards the screaming soldier clutching at his wounded leg on the ground, and kicked his weapon out of reach.

"Wait… please don't shoot," the soldier pleaded as Von pointed the rifle at his head. "If… if you let me go I'll tell you about the prisoner."

"What prisoner?" Von stomped on the man's wounded leg.

"A… a woman, in the command post. We were under orders to bring her here…"

"Why?" Von lowered his weapon, but put more weight on his leg.

"I don't know why," the man screamed, his face growing red as he writhed in agony. "I just know she's important. We set up camp while one of the others took the transport carrier to rendezvous with the *Black Bell*."

"I see." Von looked towards the large tent for a moment, considering his options, before aiming his rifle at the soldier's head.

"Wait! You said you would let me go if I talked."

"I said no such thing." Von let out a feral snarl and pulled the trigger, shooting the soldier in the head.

Von marched towards the large tent, pausing for a moment to take a breath and let his anger tapper off before stepping through the hanging flap. A large oval table covered with planetary maps, charts of the system, and a few genpads sat in the center along with a small lamp. The sound of a muffled voice drew his attention to the far corner and the young brown haired woman tied and gagged to a chair. The woman—her hazel eyes wide with fear—wore a short sapphire blue dress with a pink and blue jacket.

Not military. Von walked over to where the slender woman was bound and untied her legs and arms.

"Who are you?" The woman jumped to her feet after pulling the gag off.

"I am Von T'naat, Prince—" Pain jolting through him as he mentally corrected himself; he raised his rifle, aiming at her chest. "—King of the T'loak. What does Cole want with you?"

"Wait, don't shoot me! I'm not your enemy." Speaking with an Ethrian accent, the woman threw her hands up and tried to back away. "Those EDM goons grabbed me because Cole thinks I know the location of a secret weapons base and he doesn't."

"Do you?"

"If I said yes, would that encourage you to maybe *not* shoot me?"

"I have all of the weapons I need." Von let out a breath and lowered his rifle, turning to leave. "You're of no use to me."

"Wait." She followed him out of the tent, coughing as wave of dust blew passed. "What am I supposed to do?"

"Do as you please." Von shrugged.

"You can't just leave me out here."

"Why not?"

"Because you'd be leaving a totally helpless girl all alone on a totally fragged planet. I could be captured again, or even killed," the woman explained, her voice high and panicked. "Besides, you said you're a King didn't you? Don't you like, have to protect damsels in distress?"

"No, I don't. I have more important responsibilities than helping the helpless." Von paused by one of the dead soldiers, picked up a sword, and tossed it at the woman's feet. "If you have something to protect, take up the sword."

Moving some of her shoulder length hair out of her face, the woman glanced down at the weapon before looking back to him. "You should know that despite the stereotype that all Ethrians are master swordsmen, I've never held one before."

"Then you had best learn, or you'll die."

"Why can't I just go with you?"

"I'm T'loak. What makes you think I'm any better than your captors?" Von glanced over his shoulder and saw her standing with a nervous smile.

"You didn't shoot me."

Von stopped with a groan, surprised that a sense of guilt had swept over his anger. "You have free will, so I suppose you can choose to follow me if you want."

"You're a very angry guy aren't you?" She hurried over to his side, her smile broadening. "And my name is Lizabeth in case you were wondering."

"I wasn't."

* * *

"So what port do ya want these sent to?"

"Zion Seven, bay sixteen, and make sure they get there fast." Korso leaned against a metallic counter while the Saurian sales woman finished inputting his order into her antiquated computer. Behind him, he heard a pair of Klayvor arguing near a display terminal while a Ruetish sales woman tried to assure them the price was more than fair.

"No problem. That'll cost ya one hundred trils."

"Trils?" Korso raised an eyebrow, unfamiliar with the monetary unit. "I'm Ethrian, we don't have trils in my sector."

"Sorry, I forget all you warm bloods like standardized monies. It's equal to three hundred thirty standard credits."

"I can get the same order for half price anywhere else on the planet." Korso gestured towards the street through the tinted window, indignation lining his voice.

"Probably, but you said fast. The extra fee gets it to your port of choice within an hour."

"An hour…" Letting out a tired breath, Korso finished the order forms and paid the woman before heading outside. Walking a few yards from the door, he began to notice the lack of public traffic, when four Crimson Knights jumped from behind a parked transport and rushed towards him.

Alarm, mixed with adrenaline surged through him as he sidestepped the first Knight, clotheslining him on instinct. Before the Knight could hit the ground, another Knight tackled Korso, but as they fell, he was able to use the Knight's momentum to kick him off and into a light pillar. Rolling to his feet, he spotted the third Knight—armed with a stun baton—swinging for his head.

Korso ducked under the arching attack, only to catch a kick on the side of the head from the fourth Knight. Pain ringing his ears, he felt the sharp stab of electricity jolt through him as a baton crashed into his exposed back. Fighting to stay on his feet as he spun around, he blocked a punch from one Knight and countered with a forearm to the throat. Yanking the gaging man's weapon free, Korso shoved him aside and drove the head of the baton into the last Knight's neck and followed with a harsh uppercut to the jaw.

The sound of more yelling pilfered the small sense of relief he felt as he turned to his right and found six more Knights charging at him. *Time to go.*

Korso turned to run, finding another group of Knights blocking his path, each armed with a crackling baton. Cursing, he drew his pistols, ready to fire, but the sound of rifle safeties clicking off sent a panicked chill through him, causing him to freeze.

"I wouldn't do that if I were you." The Knight leading the second group stepped forward, gesturing with a baton towards the roofs of two buildings. "I was ordered to take you alive if possible, so I would hate to have my men shoot you now."

"So would I, Lieutenant… Tyler, if memory serves." Korso glanced up at the snipers on either side of him and cursed again as he sucked warm air back into his lungs, trying to ease the panic surging through him. Realizing he had no hope for escape, he lowered his pistols and allowed a pair of Knights to take his weapons and comm while the rest moved to surround him. "I vote for not shooting me."

Tyler smirked, stalking forward like a predator about to feast on a fat krell. "I must say, after hearing so many tales of the legendary Seraph Prime, I'm a little underwhelmed."

"Why is it people are always under or over? Why can't anyone ever just be whelmed?" Korso peered around, desperate to find a way out of their trap.

"Make this easy on yourself and tell me where your ship and the Princess are."

"Apparently you never got the memo about me." Korso forced a grin. "I have an annoying habit of being a pain in the ass."

"Not anymore." Tyler jabbed his baton into Korso's chest, sending a long wave of electricity burning through his body.

Falling to his knees, Korso looked up in time to feel a baton strike the side of his head an instant before his vision faded.

* * *

Cole sat on the lavish, and decadently comfortable, oversized throne in the Ethrian palace as a holographic image shimmered into existence a few feet in front of him. "Ah Chaple, I trust you have good news for me."

"I am afraid my Lord that I do not," Chaple answered with a bow.

"Go on." Cole leaned back, letting out an annoyed groan.

"The unit ferrying the woman made camp while waiting for our rendezvous, but when I arrived all but one was found dead, and the woman was gone."

"How?"

"It appeared to be the work of Von T'naat."

"That bastard prince is becoming more trouble than Korso." Cole rubbed the bridge of his nose, trying to stem the torrent of anger crashing against his wall of self-control. “Your priority remains the same. Continue as planned and kill Von and every tutin T’loak bastard following him with the most egregiously extreme prejudice possible.”

“Understood.”

“And should the opportunity arrive, I want you to find the girl. She is of greater importance than mere information.”

“Any preference about the survivor?” Chaple glanced to his left, undoubtedly at the soon to be dead man cowering out of the holo-emitters range.

“Failure in ones duties and cowardice while the rest of one’s unit is slain is an unforgivable offense.” Cole paused, letting a calming smile spread across his face. “But since I’m a forgiving ruler, I believe banishment is penalty enough.”

“Banishment?” Chaple raised an eyebrow, surprise lining his voice.

“Yes, just banish him… after you’ve cut out his eyes, shoved them down his throat, and sewn his mouth shut. After that, you can banish him to whatever planet side wasteland you choose. If the wild vargs don’t kill him, any T’loak that find him will.”

“As you wish, my Lord.” Chaple bowed a few moments before the hologram disappeared.

Taking a minute to enjoy the silence, Cole sat back, admiring the elaborate tapestries and various artworks hanging along the walls when a guard marched into the room and bowed.

“Forgive my intrusion, but there is a… man demanding to speak with you.”

Resting his head in his left hand, Cole stifled a tired groan. “Who is he?”

“He refused to speak with me,” the guard stated, eyes glued to the polished floor. “And I am unfamiliar with his species.”

“Really? Maybe this’ll be entertaining.” Cole punched in a few keys on the arm of his throne—making sure to keep the audio and visual off on his end—and brought up a holo of a lanky, brown scaled male, before rolling his eyes. "It's a hisser."

"Hisser, sir?"

"I forget whatever their species is actually called, but you'll understand the name in a moment." Cole activated the audio and visual, grateful that the being wasn't actually in front of him, and let his annoyance seep into his voice. "Who the hell are you and why have you bothered to waste my time?"

"I am called Karg," the man said in a deep, guttural voice. "I have called to sssee if the bounty on Rachael Ssserra ssstill ssstandsss,"

"It does. Any being that brings her to me becomes a wealthy individual."

"Then I wisssh to inform you that I have ssseen her on Secundus."

"Ah, so you've decided to annoy me with something I already know. Your only reward for that is the satisfaction of knowing that I'm going to have you shot."

Karg snorted, making what could have been an amused laugh. "And if I bring her to you, what rewardsss doesss that merit?"

"Do that, and I might be so overjoyed, I'd let you name your own reward." *Or find the best use for your skinned hide.* Cole forced a pleasant smile. Not bothering to wait for a reply, he disconnected the transmission.

"Will that be all, sire?" the guard asked, maintaining his ridged posture.

"For now." Cole waved the guard off, pleased for the first time in days. With Vega and the Hisser closing in on Korso and Rachael, one was bound to help the other kill two of the remaining obstacles that stood in the way, leaving him free to focus on saving his homeland from a fate that his predecessor failed to see. *It's a shame you wouldn't join me Korso. But then I suppose victory isn't worth much without sacrifice.*

CHAPTER SEVEN

Rachael sat on a small metal crate outside of the *Sprinthawk*, looking over the rounded docking bay for the twelfth time. *All he had to do was pick up a few crystals. No problem he said. So where is he?* Annoyed, she pushed the memory of Korso's teasing smirk from her mind and resumed tapping her foot on the tiled floor.

"Something funny?" Dee stepped down the loading ramp and flashed a knowing grin as she glanced at him, confused. "You're smiling."

"No I'm not." Rachael jump to her feet. "I was just wondering if everything was loaded."

"Ships fueled and ready to fly, save for the parts that were just delivered."

"So you haven't heard from him yet?" Rachael let a look of concern fall over her. "But then he is the most irresponsible man I've ever met."

"It's unlike him to not answer the comm's."

"So he's either goofing off, or he's in trouble." Rachael swallowed, unable to believe that Korso was childish enough to just be goofing around with the Crimson Knights chasing after them. "Can you track his comm?"

Dee pulled a small genpad from a pocket, but hesitated before looking back at Rachael. "I can, but…"

"Then let's go," Rachael cut him off before he could protest the thought of putting her in any more danger. Closing the ship's entrance, she stepped passed Dee and rushed through the spotless gray corridors of the port and onto the teeming streets. "Which way?"

"This way." Dee motioned towards her right before starting down the street. "How nice, I seem to have found a second Korso."

"I heard that." Rachael smiled, despite the apprehension she felt.

* * *

Head throbbing in pain, Korso awoke to find himself lying on the cold floor of a storage facility. He spotted a few silver crates stacked along the paneled walls as he took in his surroundings. A large freight door sat on the left side of the room while cool air blew through a smaller open door in front of him. Noticing a pair of Crimson Knights standing on either side of the doors—each armed with a pulse rifle—Korso tried to push himself up only to find his hands shackled behind him. Rolling to his knees, he glanced around again and found his weapons and comm sitting on a crate to the right. A pronounced feeling of alarm surged through him as he began to wonder what might have happened to Rachael and Dee when the sound of boots hitting concrete drew his attention towards the open door.

"Supreme Commander Korso shackled and on his knees. This is a pleasure." Vega marched in front of him followed by Tyler and a knight holding a dark case.

Korso forced a smirk, doing his best to mask the fear churning his stomach. "You kinky son of a yarl, don't go getting any strange ideas now."

"The only ideas I have involve the execution of a traitor to the Empire," Vega replied.

"I don't suppose it would do any good to tell you that I'm innocent… and you're a tool."

"No." Vega stepped over to a nearby crate and sat on top of it. "Now, I believe a debriefing is in order. Lieutenant, why don't you show him the disk."

"Yes sir." Tyler nodded towards the knight, who opened the case. A fresh wave of dread shot through Korso as Tyler pulled a black, coin sized disk out of the case. Tyler waved the two knights by the freight door over and waited for them to stand on either side of him with their weapons at the ready. "Do you know what this is?"

"If it's a suppository, I'd be more than happy to help you shove it up your ass."

"Cute. This is a rather neat device, although it was mostly unused during the war. Once attached to the base of your neck it delivers direct stimulation to the pain receptors in your body, all of them. I hear it's quite painful." Tyler walked behind him and pressed the disk into place.

Grunting through clinched teeth as the disks spines dug into his skin, Korso willed a grin back to his face despite the burning pulse tensing his neck, determined to be as difficult as possible. "You would think that sort of thing would be illegal."

Vega stood, taking a round remote from Tyler and pointed it at Korso. "Now, you will tell me everything I want to know."

"Well, my favorite color's red. My lucky number's six," Korso stated, enjoying the anger washing over Vega's face. However, his smirk faded an instant later as he fell to the floor, overwhelmed by wave of agony.

"Where is the princess?"

"I… sold her to a tribe of performing Beewa. Got four krell for her." Korso tried to force himself back to his knees, struggling to get air as his muscles spammed, but was again crippled by another jolt of blinding pain. "Funny part is… I would have done it for two."

"Where have you hidden your ship?" Vega activated the disk again, holding it for what felt like hours.

"In my pants!" Korso screamed, writhing as the disk sent wave after wave of electricity coursing through him until it felt like every bone in his body had shattered, sending flaming shards ripping through his organs.

"I don't care how long it takes but you will tell me where she is." Vega paused Korso's agony long enough to lash out with kick to his ribs.

Korso wanted to reply, to make some clever quip, but an agonized scream cut him short. Realizing after a moment that the pained shriek was his own, he tried to lash out with a kick but found himself unable to concentrate enough to move his legs. His mind and body ablaze with a pain that refused to dwindle, Korso fought to hold onto the one clear thought left to him; the only one thing that mattered.

Rachael.

* * *

Von sat on a dusty bench in front of an even dustier table deep beneath the Temple of Raj, in one of the many chambers throughout the ruined monument, staring at a worn medical pack. The circular chamber was mostly empty except for a pair of grime covered statues and a few boxes of supplies. The sound of soldiers talking and moving about in a larger chamber carried through the stone archway.

"So… why are you here in this ruined place?" Lizabeth fidgeted on the bench across from him, breaking the relative silence.

"I am here because Cole has forced me into hiding." Von reached over to the small medical pack sitting in front of him and pulled out a roll of bandages.

"So what are you gonna to do when you leave?"

"Kill Cole."

"Why? Haven't enough people died?"

"As King of the T'loak it's my duty to kill all my enemies," Von stated, wondering if his vision was blurring because of his injuries or the storm of anger that refused to subside. Turning away, he removed his shirt, wincing at the sight of the bloody bandages haphazardly wrapped around his chest.

"Why did you go to that camp to rescue me?"

"I didn't." Von began to remove his bandages with a hesitant pace, sucking in air with each ping of pain that shot through him. "I was there looking for Chaple. I had no intention of saving you."

"Oh… but you did," Lizabeth paused for a moment, and he could feel her smiling at him.

Since he had met her, she had managed to keep the same happy smile glued to her face without fail. He was beginning to wonder if she was capable of showing any other expression, but pushed aside the notion. Ethrians were arrogant by nature, but if he had to remain around one, he would resign himself to her incessant smiling. Besides, there were worst fates, and Lizabeth's smile had a calming charm that he had not yet grown tired of.

Focusing his thoughts on the task at hand, Von began to wrap his wound, an effort that proved to be more frustrating than he imagined. Growling after a second attempt, he gave up, throwing the bandages across the small room.

"You're kinda bad at that, you know."

"Do you always talk this much, or is this some kind of new Ethrian torture?" Von spun towards Lizabeth, wincing as he did.

"I'm chatty. I'm told its part of my charm." Lizabeth stood, picking up the bandages, and stepped over to Von. "Let me do it. And it wouldn't kill you to help carry on the conversation." Motioning for him to turn and face her, she pulled a bottle of disinfectant out of the med kit started to clean his wound.

"Why… why are you helping me?" Von felt himself tense as he stared at the woman, surprised to find a feeling of calmness rising within.

"Cause you look like you need it, and I've had a lot of practice."

"What do you care? Our people have been at odds with each other for decades and I have sworn to kill the man who rules your world."

"Well for starters, Cole has turned into a total tyrant, and two, like I'm really gonna sit here and watch someone suffer while I can help." Lizabeth finished with the disinfectant and began to bandage the wound. After a few minutes, she stood up, admiring her work with a smile before sitting down next to him. "All done."

"Thank you." Von returned her smile and slipped his shirt back on. Peering back towards Lizabeth, he found her staring at him and arched an eyebrow. "What?"

"I was wondering what you're like when you're not all grumpy guy."

"What?"

Lizabeth knelt in front of him. "Come on, where did you grow up? What where you like as a kid? Were you always so cranky?"

"I… you know more about me than I know of you," Von stated trying to change the subject, although not really wanting to end the conversation. "What about you, where did you grow up?"

"Me? I lived in a quiet rural area with my parents and my big brother Button, until I joined the emissary program."

"Button?" Von asked, his eye's lingering on hers.

Lizabeth smiled and began to tell Von about her childhood, but as she did, he felt himself relax for the first time since he was forced into hiding.

* * *

Rachael crept behind Dee as the pair slipped through the closing door opened by a departing employee. They had tracked Korso's comm to a small port in the eastern quarter of the city and had even managed to spot the *Crimson Sword* as it arrived. Sneaking inside, however, was proving more and more difficult. Weaving their way through the corridors while remaining unnoticed by any passing security agents was taking much longer than Rachael would have liked. Stopping to confirm they were close to reaching their goal, she handed Dee his genpad and pushed the release on the door ahead of her causing it to hiss as it slid open.

Rachael stepped into the cold room and peered around. A few florescent lights were scattered about providing minimal light for the small room. Waist high barrels with caution warnings on the side were stacked throughout the room along with a few scattered hydraulic hand carts. She spotted another door on the far side of the chamber and started towards it. "What's with the drums, extra coolant or something?"

"I believe we are in a fuel depot." Dee returned his genpad to its pocket. "One of many I'd presume."

"Don't strike a flare. Wouldn't want the place to blow up," Rachael joked.

"Done that."

"This stuff powers star-drives and you blew it up?" Rachael turned towards Dee with an incredulous stare a moment before a knowing smirk adorned her face. "Korso blew up a starport fuel depot?"

"Actually, it was my idea," Dee smirked. "It was more efficient."

"And here I thought Korso was the wild one." Rachael turned back towards the door when she felt Dee grab her arm and pull her behind a stack of barrels. An instant later, she heard the door behind them hiss open and watched two Crimson Knights stroll into view.

"I still don't see why we don't just load him onto the ship and go," one of the knights complained, slinging his rifle over his shoulder.

"Captain's orders. He probably plans to use him as bait for the other two," the second knight replied as the door hissed shut.

"Ya think they're dumb enough to come for the cachak?"

"Who knows what the traitors will do. Now shut up, some of these are ready to move."

Nodding towards Dee, Rachael stepped out from behind the crate. "Hey, were you two knuckle heads looking for me?"

Offering a playful wave to the surprised duo while Dee maneuvered around a stack of barrels to grab one of the knights from behind, Rachael grasped the collar of the second knight, sweeping his legs, and drove his head into the concrete floor. Making sure the knight was unconscious; Rachael looked back to Dee just as he punched out his opponent.

Rachael followed Dee over to one of the doors control panels and watched as he began examining it. "What are you doing?"

"Attempting to link this door with the other."

"Why?"

"So that when we make our escape, we can lock our pursuers out from the other side."

"Good idea." Rachael nodded as she started towards the door that would take her to Korso. "You get the exit ready, I'll go fetch Korso."

"Princess, I cannot let you…"

"We've been over this," Rachael stated, determination fueling every step. "I can't rig the door, but I can free Korso."

"Very well," Dee relented after a long moment.

Striding through a narrow corridor that led to a crate filled room, Rachael felt a ping of relief—one that was quickly replaced with horror—at the sight of Korso lying on the ground.

"Hey, you're not supposed to be…"

Rachael looked to her right, noticing for the first time the two knights flanking the door she had stepped through and drove her elbow into nose of a surprised knight. Spinning towards the knight on her left, she grabbed his arm as he reached for her and used it to pull him off balance while shoving his head against wall. Not giving him the chance to recover, Rachael swept his legs out from under him and dropped her shin onto his throat the instant he hit the ground.

"Shoot her!"

Rachael's attention snapped towards the other side of the room and the woman raising her rifle along with two more knights.

"Hold fire." Tyler stepped between the pair of knights. "Our orders are to capture her alive."

Rachael glared at Tyler, fury burning her face, as she drew her sword. "Leave now and I might just be gracious enough to forget you ever existed when I assume the throne."

"I don't think so. I wanted you alive, but if you refuse to cooperate, injured is just as good." Tyler motioned towards Rachael, which sent the two knights flying towards her with their swords in hand.

Her own sword springing to life as she meet their advance, Rachael ducked under an arching attack and parried another. Keeping her weapon moving—whether it was to defend or attack—she kept her opponents off balance, staying in constant motion as she danced around or between them, not wanting to allow them enough time for an effective counter attack.

Rachael parried a thrust from the male knight, shoving him into a large crate as she did, and spun towards the woman, catching her with a kick the chest. Pressing her advantage, Rachael spun on the opposite foot and blocked a defensive swing before punching the woman on the jaw an instant before her blade found the woman's belly.

Yanking her weapon free from the slain knight, Rachael turned in time to see the other kick her in the stomach, which sent her stumbling into a stack of crates. Scrambling to regain her balance while blocking his follow up attack, she spun behind him, swiping her sword across his lower back. Crying out in pain, the knight lashed out with a blind swing as he turned, but was felled with a quick slash to the throat.

“Nicely done.” Tyler hit her with the back of his fist and launched a series of fluid attacks.

Ducking and weaving as fast as she could, Rachael caught Tyler’s blade with a downward parry and tried to spin behind him, but the older knight matched her maneuver, and replied with a harsh elbow. His lips curling into a self-satisfied smirk, Tyler pressed forward, driving home a growing sense of fear with every near miss. Tyler lunged with an arcing strike, only to have it deflected as she twirled her sword and nailed him with a satisfying back-fist, but as he stumbled back, he caught her with a glancing cut to the left arm.

Nerves singing from red-hot pain, Rachael forced her growing fatigue from her mind and pushed forward with a flurry of strikes, most of which were blocked. She aimed a thrust at Tyler’s chest, but he managed to catch her arm and spun her into one of the crates. Giving her just enough time to bounce off the metal cube, Tyler pounced on top of her, attempting to use her stomach as a sheath.

Desperation fueling her muscles while she fought to hold him back, Rachael managed to kick one of his legs out from under him and rolled off the crate. Falling on top of Tyler, she let out a frantic shout, driving her sword into his shoulder, and unleashed a harsh punch to the face as he cried out. She reached back to hit him again, however, he managed to knock her off with a blow of his own. Yanking her sword free, Tyler began to rise, sucking in ragged breaths, but Rachael unloaded a savage kick, driving the heel of her boot into his nose. Lungs burning and her muscles screaming from fatigue as she scrambled to her feet, she kicked him again, causing the knight to fall limp.

“Cachak!” Rachael kicked Tyler again, venting her anger, and scanned the room, hopping there were no other knights to assist him. Breathing heavily, she scooped up her sword, trying to push back the fright still shaking her hands.

Korso!

Rachael ran around the crates blocking her path and found Korso sitting upright, staring with a haggard, yet somehow cocky grin. "Okay, I'm impressed."

Rachael failed to hide her delight as she retracted her blade and returned it to her belt before knelling in front of him. "You should be. I had excellent tutors, or did you think I carried this for show?"

"Well, yeah." Korso shrugged.

"You arrogant pigheaded jerk. Why did I bother saving your worthless caz? I risk my life and you can't even say: *thanks Rachael, thank you for saving my life*. And you look horrible by the way."

"Have I mentioned how glad I am I brought you with me, and I didn't know you cared."

"You can stand to mention it a bit more, and I don't care… much."

"Good to know." Korso smiled, holding up his hands. "Now, do you mind untying me and getting this thing off my neck?"

"What did they do to you?" Rachael looked at the disk on his neck, unsure if she really wanted the answer.

"Never mind that, over by the door there's a case with the key's and a three pronged claw thingy."

Rachael hurried over to where he had pointed and grabbed the claw and key's, but her attention was drawn to the twelve knights running down the corridor opposite her and punched the door's release button, closing it before pushing another to lock it. A familiar sense of dread began to return while she ran back, released the shackles binding Korso's hands, and handed him the claw.

Korso shook his head and pushed it back to her, his face pale. "I need you to do it."

"I can't, I don't know how."

"We ain't got time for this Rachael. That door won't hold for long and I got no intention of being interrogated by the Crimson

Banas again." Korso groaned, rolling to his knees. "All you gotta do is position the claw, push the button, and yank the thing out."

"Won't that hurt you?"

"Like a kick in the crouch, now do it," Korso demanded, his voice weak.

Biting back her own fear, Rachael positioned the claw and closed her eyes, swallowing before yanking the disk free from his neck. Fearing that she might have hurt him worse as he cried out from pain and blood poured from his neck, she knelt beside him. "Sorry."

"Thanks." Korso pointed towards his weapons on the crate across from him. "Grab my gear. I'd say it's time to go."

Handing him his weapons belt, Rachael pulled his arm over her shoulder as he rose on shaky legs, keenly aware of the knights prying open the door and Tyler stirring by the crates. Moving as fast as they could, she helped Korso hobble through the corridor she had used earlier and into the fuel depot just as Tyler began barking orders to pursue.

"Cut them off." Rachael hurried through the open door that led to Dee and the rest of the facility.

Korso spun towards Dee. "Wait. Did I see fuel drums?"

"Yeah, so…"

"The room shielded?"

"Indeed." Dee nodded, catching on to something she missed.

"Good. Don't close the door until I say so." Korso turned to face the approaching knights and pulled a small ruby colored oval from his belt.

"What are you doing? We don't have time for this?" Rachael stated, her voice high and frantic.

Stopping halfway through the fuel room, the dozen knights aimed their rifles while Tyler stormed past, holding his bleeding shoulder. "I may get reprimanded for having you shot, but rest assured I will if you don't surrender now."

"What are ya doing?" Rachael repeated with a growing sense of distress as Dee's story popped back into her mind.

"Getting a bana off my back." Korso flashed a malicious grin while twisting the top of the grenade and tossed it at Tyler's feet. "Now."

Entering a command into the panel, Dee sealed the door—trapping the knights inside—while Korso offered a mock salute. A second later, the entire complex trembled as the grenade detonated, knocking Rachael and the others off their feet with a deafening roar while setting off emergency alarms throughout the complex.

"What the yanz was that?" Rachael spun towards Korso, more surprised than furious.

"Contingency plan number two," Korso answered with a weak but lopsided grin.

Rachael resisted the urge to kick him and helped Korso to his feet again. "You're out of your mind. You could have been blown us all up."

"Relax, it's all part of the plan."

"We should hurry before they seal off the area." Dee stood and started towards the exit. Following behind him, they made their way back outside and found a parked transport truck in the back lot.

"And what's next in this master plan of yours?" Rachael helped Korso climb in while Dee began to bypass the ignition safety.

"I'm open to suggestions."

"I vote for running." Rachael smiled, climbing in next to him.

Korso tried to laugh but only managed a painful groan. "Running's not a plan, remember?"

Rachael couldn't help but laugh again, comforted by Korso's cocky smirk and ecstatic that he was alive and out of danger. "Shut up."

* * *

"You had better have good news, Captain." Cole's voice carried an ominous undertone—even over the bridge speakers and the murmur of the crew occupying themselves with whatever task they could find—as his holographic image appeared in front of Vega.

"Lord Cole, I am pleased to report that we have captured Korso." Vega clasped his hands behind his back to keep them from fidgeting, wishing he had taken the transmission in his office.

"And the Princess?"

"We have begun questioning him now. It's shouldn't be long before he tells us where the Princess is."

Cole rolled his eyes with an irritated growl before returning his gaze to Vega. "Captain, Korso would never willingly betray an ally and you're far too incompetent to break him. If Hestron interrogators couldn't do the job, what makes you think you have the tools to do it? Find Rachael or…" He trailed off as a loud explosion shook the docking bay floor, sending an ear jarring rumble reverberating through the ship. "What was that?"

Vega stood frozen, trying to get a grasp of what was happening while alarms began wailing and the crew became frenzied, shouting readings from terminals. "I'm not sure."

"Well here's a suggestion, and there's no hurry or anything, but maybe you should find out! I'll wait."

"Yes sir." Vega snapped to attention while the image of Cole sat on the throne. Turning on his heel towards the helmsman yelling into a comm, he took a long steading breath. "Report."

"We're getting all kinds of comm traffic sir. All we've been able to confirm is that there was an explosion ground side, the prisoner hasn't been found, and Lieutenant Tyler isn't responding."

"Find out everything you can," Vega ordered. Those last words hit him like a knife in the gut as he realized that Korso was probably gone and with him, his single chance to avoid Cole's ever growing disdain for failure.

"Captain, preliminary reports from port control." Lira strode across the CIC and handed him a report. "And Lord Cole has asked for an update."

Scanning through the report, which only added to his growing fear, Vega tried to focus on conveying a composed air of command. "Thank you Lieutenant." He gave her a quick nod and stepped back into the range of the holo-projectors.

Cole sat with his chin resting on his fist, tapping his fingers on his free hand, his features neutral except for his eyes. Even over the vast distance between systems, Vega could feel the seething fury pouring out and wished he was somewhere, anywhere, but trapped in their gaze. "Well?"

"It… it appears that Korso has escaped… for the moment." Vega paused, waiting for Cole to begin screaming at him, but all he got was a cold stare. "During his escape, he detonated some fuel tanks."

"I see." Cole continued to hold that same chilling stare. After what seemed to be an eternity, Cole's gaze shifted to the right. "And you are?"

"Lieutenant M'gaan Lira, sir." Lira snapped to attention.

"Lieutenant, escort Vega to the brig and bring him to me."

"Lord Cole, please, I will find Korso and the Princess again. Give me a final chance," Vega pleaded. He waited, unable to keep his body from shaking, while Cole appeared to consider something, and to his surprise—and dismay—Cole smiled. It was an eerie smile. One that could make even the most seasoned soldier's spine tingle with fear.

"Since I am a forgiving Emperor, and you have served the Empire faithfully, I'll allow you a second chance to redeem yourself. However, there will not be a third, and you won't like what happens if you fail again." Cole spoke in a calm, disturbing voice, one that quieted the buzz of bridge activity. "Lieutenant, should Vega fail again, you are to relieve him from command and return to Ethria."

"Yes sir," Lira said with a bow. After a second Cole's image disappeared and Vega was left standing humiliated, cowering like a small child. "Your orders Captain?"

It took him a few seconds to snap out of his own thoughts, all of which told him he was as good as dead already, and turned towards the ambitious woman. "Find the transport they stole." He attempted to regain his composure and sat down in the command chair, watching Lira begin to relay the order, and noting the new found swagger in her voice.

* * *

Korso grimaced as Dee pulled their stolen transport to a sudden stop outside of the port that housed the *Sprinthawk*. Letting Dee run ahead to start the checkout process, he climbed out of the truck with Rachael's help, mindful of every pain inducing step.

"I'll be glad to get off this rock," Rachael said as they followed Dee towards their docking bay.

"Told you this place was fun," Korso replied dryly.

"Oh shut up."

Rachael continued to help him as they worked their way through the dingy corridors. He felt out of place needing to be helped like this, however, he didn't mind having Rachael close around. Wondering when he had started to think of her as anything more than an inherited pain, he noticed that she was staring at him with an expectant look. "Huh?"

"I asked what you're smiling about now."

"Nothing." He looked away for a moment. "You guys get the stuff for the fold-generator?"

"We did, but we didn't have time to install the components." Dee stopped and held the next door open for Korso and Rachael. "We'll have to fix as we fly."

"With the knights distracted, it should be clear sailing out of here." Korso and Rachael stepped into the next room—which was somewhat empty save for a few waiting chairs, a small table, lights, and the pair of scale covered Strien aiming crossbows at them—and cursed in unison. "Or not."

"Good to sssee you not captured by knightsss in crimssson." The lankier of the two smiled, flashing a mouth full of fangs.

"Today has not been one of my better days," Korso groaned, stepping forward at the shorter, darker ones order. "And what smells like a latrine?"

"I believe they call it perfume," Dee responded, his body tensing, ready to attack.

"Quiet. No more talk. Ethriansss alwaysss talk too much." The lanky one motioned towards the door that opened into the docking bay and waited for them to step through. "Tarful, you ssshoot them if they try anything."

"Ready to do it now, Karg. Easssier that way when we take their ssship."

Rachael shared a glance with Korso for a moment before letting go of his arm. "Or..." Pivoting to her side, she nailed Tarful with a kick to the stomach while drawing her pistol.

Dee shot forward, landing an elbow on Karg, drawing his own pistol, just as Korso pulled his free. An uncomfortable silence fell over the hanger, as the two Strien managed to recover enough to re-aim their weapons—their bows trained on Korso and Rachael and a knife on Dee's throat—causing everyone to freeze.

"Drop your weapons," an unfamiliar voice ordered, breaking the silence along with a symphony of rifles charging and swords unfolding. "Now!"

Korso shifted his gaze away from the bow pointed at his head and found himself surrounded by ten T'loak soldiers and hastily drew his second pistol. "Oh hell."

"Thisss not concern you." Karg shifted his aim towards the blond haired man. "Leave, now."

"I have you surrounded and outnumbered, *and* I'm offering you the chance to leave with your lives," the familiar looking man aimed his own pistol at Karg. "I'd take it."

"You mean them?" Korso gestured to the two Strien, realization widening his eyes in surprise, and backed away along with Rachael and Dee. "We'll just clear your line of fire."

"You not ssstop usss T'loak…"

"Shoot them." The blond man unleashed two plasma rounds, hitting Karg on the chest while the rest of his men gunned down Tarful.

Korso kept his pistols trained on the blond man as the squad of T'loak turned towards the Ethrians. "You seem somewhat familiar, have I held a gun on you before?"

"We've met briefly. My name is Orrin T'zael. I serve King Von." He offered a warm smile, returning his weapon to its holster.

Korso winced, noting the pain shooting through his ribs as he kept his weapon up. "Ain't that special."

"What do you want with us?" Dee asked.

Orrin took a cautious step forward, holding up his hands. "I have come for Princess Rachael."

"Prepare to be disappointed." Korso stepped in front of Rachael, ready to shoot.

"You misunderstand." Orrin motioned for his men to lower their weapons. "Lord Von wishes to *meet* with the Princess to discuss an alliance to defeat Cole."

"Last time we met, you tried to throw us into a pool of tutin lava," Korso stated.

"I promise you that she will be safe."

Rachael stepped past Korso and pushed his arm down. "I'll go with you."

"What?" Korso stared at her with an incredulous look.

"There's no way we can overthrow Cole by ourselves, but maybe with their help we can." Rachael held his arm. "And if they wanted us dead, they could have shot us already."

"She has a point." Dee stepped up to Korso's side. "We should at least hear what they have to say."

"Why not," Korso mumbled, as he looked back at Orrin. "But if she goes, we all go."

"Of course, you and General Dee are both welcome," Orrin amended.

Korso started to reply, but winced as Vega's voice boomed over the faculty intercom. "This is Captain Vega of the Crimson Knights, ordering the immediate and unconditional surrender of Rachael Serra and her confederates. Resist in any way, and I level this complex."

"He's awfully cranky." Korso peered around, half expecting a squad of knights to pop out.

"Princess we should leave immediately. My ship is in the next hanger," Orrin stepped over towards Rachael.

"Like hell. We're taking the *Sprinthawk.* If you wanna tag along, fine." Korso started to limp his way towards the ship and opened the access hatch.

"What should we do?" a soldier asked as he stepped forward.

"Get back to the shuttle and see if you can stall the Crimson Knights. I will go with the Princess and we can rendezvous at the temple." Orrin followed them up the ramp just as the first volley of ion cannon fire rocked the port.

Sealing the hatch, Korso hobbled behind Dee and the others up to the bridge, grunting from pain as he bounced off a bulkhead, cursing as another near miss shook the complex. "Time to go."

"You're in no condition to fly right now," Rachael stated, concern lining her voice.

"Can't argue with that," Korso admitted.

"I can fly us out of here." Orrin started for the pilot's seat only to freeze mid-step as Korso pointed one of his pistols at him.

"No one flies my ship but me and Dee, or Rachael, got it?"

"Apologies." Orrin backed away from the chair with his hand up.

Korso pointed to the comm station and returned his weapon to its holster. "Now sit there and don't touch anything. Rachael, take the weapons. Dee, you fly."

"Me?" Rachael glanced towards him, surprise widening her eyes, before sitting next to Dee in the co-pilot's seat.

"I assume you know how." Korso started towards the engine room. "I'll get the fold-generator going."

"And where are we supposed to fly too?" Rachael began to bring the ships system online.

"Head for Farina in the Chubarae system," Orrin answered.

Leaving the bridge, Korso hobbled his way to the engine room as fast as his injuries would allow—stopping to steady himself as the ship left the port and find the components he had ordered—and hurried to the fold generator, sliding the control panel open. He tore through the container holding the crystal, praying that his beloved ship would hold together since he didn't have time to install the other components.

Ignoring the muffled thumps of ion blasts hammering the shields, Korso slid the crystal into place and let out a relieved breath as it hummed to life. It was a reassuring hum, one that had saved his life more times than he would have preferred.

The ship banked starboard, hard, launching Korso into another bulkhead and sending a fresh reminder of his injuries surging through him. Moving over to the interior comm, he thumbed it on and was greeted by Rachael's angelic voice, cursing with words even he had never heard before.

"The *Crimson Sword* is closing, we need to fold, now," Dee stated.

"Feel free to go anytime, we're good—relatively speaking." Korso smiled, bracing himself for the sudden vertigo as the fold-generator propelled the ship into hyperspace. *That's my girl.*

* * *

Vega let out a defeated, hopeless breath as the *Sprinthawk* disappeared in a flashing streak of green light, and with it, his last chance for salvation. Turning away from the forward screen, he saw Lira and three knights stepping over with weapons in hand.

"Captain, by the authority of Emperor Cole, I formally relive you of command." Lira plucked his sword from his belt and handed it to one of the knights. "For the sake of morale, I trust you'll make this transition as easy as possible."

"Very well." Vega took a long, deep breath, forcing himself to keep his head high and started towards the lift. Knowing that there was nowhere to run on the ship, his only remaining hope was that he would somehow die with some manner of dignity, but deep down he realized all he could expect was a painful end to a loyal and well-decorated career.

CHAPTER EIGHT

The *Sprinthawk* sat in a long abandoned military base on the far side of the second of four moons orbiting Farina. Remembering how much time he had spent fighting Hestron troops and wondering where they were getting their constant reinforcements from, Korso couldn't help but laugh at the irony of using their old base to hide from his own people floating on the opposite side of the planet. The fact that he had never found the place made him feel a bit more reassured about leaving his ship, but he still didn't like the idea. Especially since the T'loak had taken it over; and he still wasn't quite ready to trust them yet.

Korso peered across the cavernous hanger and found Orrin talking to one of his soldiers and tried to figure out what they were saying. Giving up after a few seconds, he stepped over to Rachael while Dee started down the *Sprinthawk's* ramp.

"I am afraid that the fold-generator and shield array will require some work before we are able to leave," Dee said.

"I figured as much, but I'm sure you can get it fixed in a few hours?"

Dee turned towards Korso with a raised eyebrow. "My previous engineering handy work aside, you are aware that I'm not a literal miracle worker aren't you?"

"Consider my ignorance a testament to your phenomenal skill." Korso motioned over to the pair of T'loak. "Besides, Orrin offered to have someone help with the repairs, but I don't want them poking around alone."

"You still don't trust him?" Rachael asked.

"Not entirely." Korso shrugged.

"How are we supposed to form an alliance if you act like a distrustful immature jerk?" Rachael glared at Korso.

"After the couple of days it took to get here, I'm willing to accept that they're not planning to kill us, so I got no problem working with the T'loak, but trust takes time. You wanna cut a deal with Prince *has a large rock firmly lodged up his backside*; I won't get in your way. And I'm not immature."

"Well it's good to see you're feeling better, and you are immature."

"I'm not."

"You are."

"Please." Dee held up his hands with a smirk. "You both are."

Korso started to reply but was cut short as Orrin walked over with a soldier. "Adan will see to any repairs your ship requires," Orrin said. "We can take a shuttle down to the planet."

"I'll show him where to start." Dee motioned towards the open hatch. "One treaty with Korso was enough for me."

Korso held up his arms as if he were hurt. "Always a quip with you."

"And he says we're immature," Rachael added.

"Which we're not." Korso held Rachael's smile for a moment before turning towards Orrin, who was staring with a raised eyebrow. "What? We're not."

"If you're ready?" Orrin pointed to a small short range shuttle.

"We are." Rachael pushed Korso forward and followed Orrin into the cramped shuttle. "Ready, I mean. Not the other thing."

"Smooth." Korso sat on the bench like seat next to her while Orrin instructed the pilot to take off.

"Oh shut up."

The shuttle left the hanger and made planetary entry with the usual chop expected from vessels with little to no inertial dampeners. Finding a place to land in the ruined city of Adom, Korso stared through the tinted view port, struggling against the memories that boiled to the surface. Flashes of moments spent fighting for survival, memories of friends dying, and of enduring some of the worst moments of his life at the side of his friend filled his thoughts even as he closed his eyes, trying to push them back with every breath.

Exiting the shuttle, Orrin led them through the city to what was now known as the Temple of Raj. With the exception of years of dust and cobwebs covering the sand colored stone walls, the temple was just as Korso remembered: a never ending series of maze like corridors with little to no light and stuffy underground chambers. The deeper they walked, he spotted more and more T'loak soldiers, many of which stopped whatever they were doing to stare as Korso and Rachael passed by.

"Lord Von is through here." Orrin looked over his shoulder and paused next to a grime covered archway before gesturing for them to go ahead.

Korso followed Rachael into the small chamber, only to have his attention drawn to Von and the woman sitting on the dusty table. Eyes widening in surprise, followed by an eruption of anger that made his head feel light, he ripped a pistol free of its holster, leveling it at Von. "What the *yanz* is she doing here?"

"Button!" Lizabeth turned with a wide smile and scrambled over the table, wrapping her arm around him, excitement raising her voice.

"Button?" Rachael, Von, and Orrin gasped in unison, each mirroring the confused expressions of the others.

Korso ignored the wave of embarrassment that washed over him, as well as the ache from his sides, and pried Lizabeth off before glaring at Von. "If you hurt her—I don't care how many soldiers you got out there—I shoot you now."

"Relax Alex, it's not like that." Lizabeth smiled again after kicking his shin. "Von saved me."

"She was being held prisoner by Chaple when I found her," Von said, rising to his feet.

Lizabeth shrugged. "His EDM goons grabbed me while I was working on Secundus and dragged me here."

"*You* were his mystery package?" Korso laughed, understanding why Cole had gone to such lengths to hide what was being delivered. It was a realization, and betrayal, that infuriated him all over again.

"I'm sorry, but who is she again?" Rachael looked from Lizabeth to him.

Realizing that Lizabeth wasn't in danger, Korso swallowed and returned his weapon to his belt, hoping to hide his reddening face. "She's my younger sister."

"Wait, you have a sister?" Rachael laughed. "Who apparently calls you Button?"

"We are so *not* talking about that." Korso shot Rachael a glare, embarrassment and annoyance warming his face. "Now can we please just do what we came here to do?"

"Lord Von, the Princess has agreed to negotiate a treaty." Orrin walked over to Von's side still eyeing the siblings.

"Have a seat." Von sat down, motioning for the others to do the same while glancing between Lizabeth and Korso with an arched eyebrow. Rachael sat opposite of Von and looked over at Korso as if she was waiting for him to sit.

"Don't look at me." Korso waved his hands and leaned back against the wall with his sister. "If I learned anything from the war, it's that getting involved with one negotiation was enough."

"So where do we start?" Rachael asked.

"Cole is the reason we're in hiding. Cole is the reason our fathers are dead, and he is intent on killing us both. I say we start by plunging a dagger into his heart," Von stated, his voice low and cold.

"Agreed." Rachael nodded. "But I don't want to kill innocent people just to get to Cole."

"Princess, anyone willing to follow Cole is not innocent," Von scuffed.

"Maybe, but the citizens of Ethria are, and I refuse to see them hurt along with the guilty." Rachael leaned forward, lacing her fingers together, and adopted the same posture Korso had seen her father use whenever he refused to budge on a subject. "Any action we take has to have minimal effect on civilians."

"A surgical strike then. We get in, neutralize any resistance, and kill Cole," Von paused, thinking over something. "The problem is I don't have the man power for a full blitz. Not against the most fortified planet in the Ethrian Empire."

"Unfortunately, the only one willing to help me is over there." Rachael gestured towards Korso.

"About that." Korso turned towards the table, kicking himself for not remembering earlier. "Back on Secundus, I ran into someone who used to be under my command. As it turns out, Cole has somewhat overstated the strength of his military force."

"And you just now think to tell me this?" Rachael snapped her head around, anger narrowing her eyes.

"It slipped my mind, what with the torture and all." Korso waved his hands. "Point is, I know where we can pick up a few platoons of loyal Ethrians itching to stick it to Cole."

"That changes things." Rachael turned back to Von. "So what happens after Cole is gone?"

"My concern is killing Cole and protecting my people, not in conquering Ethria," Von replied. "Once he's dead, we go our separate ways."

"Lord Von, Princess Rachael." Orrin stepped to where they both could see him. "Forgive my interruption, but you cannot just let your alliance end that way."

"What do you mean?" Von looked at Orrin, surprised.

"Ethria and the T'loak are two of the most dominant powers in the sector and make up the bulk of humanity in the galaxy, but we've been locked in a pointless cold war for so long no one remembers how it started. We're always looking for an excuse to fight simply because it's become tradition—a tradition that's left both our worlds vulnerable to men like Cole—but we can be so much more." Orrin glanced from Von to Rachael, leaning on the table. "*You* could make us so much more.

"A permanent alliance between our nations could allow both to recover from a decade of meaningless wars. Alone, we'll all struggle and die, or be easy targets for some other world. If we can live together, you can give us an era of peace that our worlds have long since stopped believing was possible. One that finally unites mankind, and shows the rest of the galaxy that we're not a bunch of feuding warlords too foolish to stop bickering amongst ourselves; we're something to be feared." Orrin sucked in a long breath, clasping his hands behind his back as he regained his composure. After a long, uncomfortable minute, he turned back towards Von. "I am sorry, Lord Von. I know it's not my place…"

Von stood, cutting Orrin off, and placed a hand on his shoulder with what might have passed for a smile. "Orrin believes that our alliance should be permanent, and I trust his judgment. And if Orrin trusts you, then I will gladly join you in an alliance."

"My father always told me that humanity would either learn to live together, or we'd die alone in the dark." Rachael stood and extended her hand, smiling. "I would be honored to live beside you."

"I so wish I had a holo-recorder," Lizabeth whispered. "This was kinda big, huh?"

"And Dee missed it." Korso laughed, crossing his arms. "He'd probably say something about her father being proud."

"Sounds like you're proud." Lizabeth nudged Korso with her elbow.

"A little." Korso smiled, holding his gaze on Rachael. "And I'll bet Cole won't see this coming."

* * *

After hours of discussion, Rachael and Von had come to terms and adjourned for the evening, freeing Korso to wander around the ancient temple. Light from T'loak glow rods reflected off the golden statues scattered throughout the vast chamber turned camp, giving the hall a pleasant, inviting feel. The murmur of soldiers conversing about Rachael and Von's new alliance echoed throughout the camp with surprising acceptance—a startling testament towards their faith in their new King as much as their desire to see Cole deposed. A desire Korso intended to see fulfilled.

Veering up a winding ramp, Korso found his sister and Rachael sitting on a balcony overlooking the chamber, laughing as if they had known each other for years. *Well, this can't be good.*

"Hi… Button." Rachael turned and waved with a twisted smile. "Lizabeth and I were just talking about you."

"No, no… this stops now. No calling me Button." Korso shifted his annoyed gaze to Lizabeth. "No embarrassing stories and no talking. Talking is bad, so stop."

"What's wrong, you can quip it out but you can't take it?" Rachael asked, reveling in the embarrassment on his face. "You know, you're kinda cute when you're flustered."

"Cute?" Korso looked away for a moment, unable to suppress his smile. "I'm a soldier, not cute."

Lizabeth glanced from Rachael to Korso and jumped to her feet, her smile widening as she stepped over to his side. "Oh… you totally have the hot's for her don't you?"

"What? Me… her… I'm not answering that. I banned talking remember?"

"Come on, tell me. I already know you do, so you might as well answer." Lizabeth shook his arm, reminding him of when they were kids.

"Yeah Korso." Rachael crossed her arms. "Answer the question."

Korso glanced at each of them, before letting out a defeated breath. "You two are enjoying this aren't you?"

"Doesn't suck," Rachael replied.

"Yep." Lizabeth leaned in close to Korso. "I like her, and you obviously do too, so don't blow it."

"I'm not…"

"Just be nice, ok?" Lizabeth stepped behind him and nudged him forward before starting down the ramp. "I'm going to go find Von."

"Hey," Korso called after her. "You're awfully chummy with him. When do we get to talk about that?"

"Bye." Lizabeth waved without turning around.

Korso turned back towards Rachael, who was grinning from ear to ear, and let out a tired sigh. "Okay, I'm only gonna say this once, don't call me Button. I really hate that name."

"Sure, whatever you say." Rachael shrugged. "But I can learn a lot from her when it comes to pushing your buttons."

"I'd take it as a kindness if you didn't." Korso sat down next to Rachael and took in the golden hue of the chamber below. "Look, I never thanked you for saving me back on Secundus, so thanks."

"You call that a thank you?" Rachael asked, pretending to be hurt. "You could put a little more feeling into it. Let's see some of that cute as a button innocence you used to have."

"I can't believe Liz told you that."

"Yeah." Rachael chuckled. She leaned back on her hands, considering something, as they listened to murmur of the soldiers. "Back on Secundus you called me Rachael."

"Well, that is your name isn't it?"

"It's just… that was the first time you ever called me by name."

"Really?" Korso caught her gaze, unsure about how to respond. "Probably just a slip of the tongue. I can go back to calling you the imperial bratness."

"You never called me that." Rachael pushed him with a smirk.

"I was getting to that one, eventually."

"Doesn't matter. I kinda like the sound of my name on your lips," she replied, running her fingers along the side of her neck.

They sat in silence for a few minutes, giving Korso time to wonder when his feelings for Rachael had begun to change. *I hate when Liz is right.*

"So why'd you let me help fly your ship?" Rachael asked, breaking the silence.

"I figured you could handle it. You seemed pretty confident you could fly her when we first met." Enjoying the warmth of her smile, Korso let his gaze linger on hers. "You're the only person besides Dee who I've ever let fly her."

"I guess that means you're starting to trust me."

"Apparently."

"So what was it like living in rural Ethria?"

"Extremely boring." Korso leaned back. "That's why I joined the military in the first place."

"Lizabeth said that your father didn't like the idea."

"He was furious, which made it all the more better. He wanted me to do as he did and crunch numbers, but all I wanted to do was see the stars, have an adventure or two. Of course, I didn't expect to be fighting in a war for all those years." He found himself surprised that he was telling her all this since he never talked about his past.

Holding her gaze for a long moment, they started to lean towards each other when a movement from the ramp caused them to look over and see Orrin walking up.

"Forgive my interruption Princess, but Lord Von wishes to speak with you and Korso."

Just when we were starting to get along. Korso shifted towards the stiff man, letting his annoyance slip into his voice. "Great."

"Lead the way." Rachael let out an annoyed laugh and stood.

Climbing to his feet, Korso followed them through the varying corridors until they reached a side entrance to the temple and stepped out to find Lizabeth standing with Von. A moment later a black topless repulser-car pulled in front of them.

"Anything else Lord Von?" The soldier driving the transport hopped out.

"Tell the other's to start packing. Once the Princess and I return, we'll be leaving," Von answered.

"Where we going?" Korso asked.

"I have a caravan with weapons and supplies coming through the old capital and I wanted to ensure it arrives unencumbered," Von replied. "I assumed you all would want to come along."

"Might as well." Rachael climbed in behind Orrin.

Korso started to jump in next to Rachael but stopped when Lizabeth beat him to the seat. "Liz, what are you doing?"

"I'm going with you." Lizabeth gave a nonchalant shrug. "What's it look like I'm doing?"

"No you're not, it's too dangerous."

"He is right." Von took the seat next to Orrin and looked back. "Chaple's men may still be looking for you."

"I'm as safe with a King, a soldier, and my sword wielding overprotective brother as I am in some dusty old temple," Lizabeth stated.

"Fine," Korso conceded after a moment and sat next to her. "But you're staying in the transport the whole time, got it?"

Lizabeth smiled just as Orrin pulled away from the temple. Flying a few feet above the ground as they sped towards what was left of Adom, Korso began to wish he had made her stay once she started telling Rachael more about their childhood as they neared the city. Stone from fallen walls and buildings, scorched black by plasma fire and ion canons, covered the streets of Adom. An arid breeze kicked up clouds of charred dirt giving the dark brownish sky an even more depressing look than Korso remembered. The only difference he could see was the fact that the Hestrons weren't trying to kill him—at least for the moment—but Cole was, and once again Korso was faced with the possibility that the people he cared for the most might die on this twice forsaken planet.

Pushing memories and anger aside, Korso caught the tail end of his sister's conversation with Von just as Orrin pulled the transport next to the partial remains of a building.

"All of this happened during the war?" Lizabeth followed Rachael out of the transport.

"To be fair, it was a piss hole before then too." Korso hopped to the ground only to get slapped on the back of the head by Rachael.

"Behave."

"It was." Korso gestured towards Von and Orrin, who were both pulling a pulse rifle from the back compartment of the transport, while avoiding another swing from Rachael. "And they think so too. I can see it in their eyes. They have the look of men stuck someplace they have no intention of staying."

"I'm sure it was downright pretty once," Lizabeth stated, following close to Von.

"He's right." Von peered over the remnants of the city. "My people abandoned the city to the Hestrons years ago only to watch them abandon it during the war. The city is little more than a blood soaked marker of pointless death."

"See, piss hole." Korso followed Orrin and the others through what once might have been an alley and onto a dirt covered street.

"You really don't like this city, do you?" Rachael asked, her voice soft.

"Really don't," Korso replied, eager to forget about all the time he and Cole had spent on the planet.

They walked the rest of way in silence, cutting through buildings or alleys whenever toppled ruins obstructed their path. Finding their way onto yet another debris filled street, they started towards what remained of a large, elegant structure.

"Is that them?" Rachael pointed towards a trio of parked transport trucks near the building.

"Yes," Orrin replied, sharing a confused look with Von. "But they should…"

"Chaple." Von clicked the safety off his rifle as a look of rage fell over him. Following his gaze to the top of the building ahead of them, Korso found Chaple staring down at them.

"I am afraid, Prince Von, you missed your caravan. However, I am certain Lord Cole will find some use for the supplies." Chaple shifted his stoic gaze to Rachael. "My apologies Princess, but I was not expecting to see you or I would have planned a more fitting welcome. Regardless, by order of your Emperor, you are all hereby bound by law. Lay down your arms and surrender."

"Your Emperor, not mine." Korso whipped one of his pistols out only hear the hum of multiple pulse rifles arming. Peering around, he counted over a dozen EDM soldiers popping out from behind cover.

"If you care at all about the lives of your cohorts Princess, I would strongly advise them to surrender," Chaple stated.

"Go suck dren from a quan," Rachael spat.

Chaple titled his head, feigning confusion. "Resist and you die."

"You first." Von fired a volley of plasma rounds, forcing Chaple to duck out of the way. An instant later, a torrent of enemy fire rained over the street, compelling Korso and the others to find cover.

Diving alongside Von behind the overturned carcass of a transport, Korso spared a hasty glance, searching for Rachael. "Where's Rachael and Liz?"

Von leaned around the side of the transport, answering the soldier's second barrage with one of his own. "They're with Orrin on the other side of the street."

Spotting Rachael and Orrin returning fire from behind a half crumbled wall on the far side of the street with Lizabeth, Korso clicked on his comm. "Yo, Rach?"

"Kinda busy at the moment," Rachael replied, still firing.

Korso ducked back behind cover, avoiding a string of plasma. "Can you guys get back to the transport from over there?"

"I think so," Rachael replied.

"Then get going. We'll meet you there."

"And let you get captured again?"

"Not the time to argue. Get going."

"You'd better not keep me waiting," Rachael exclaimed after a long moment. Waiting until the three of them disappeared into another building, Korso resigned himself to keeping Chaple's goons off their backs long enough to make their escape, and joined Von in another volley.

"We have to go." Von unloaded another set of plasma rounds before starting down the street to their right.

Shooting blindly at the pursuing soldiers as Korso followed Von from cover to cover—all while trying to ignore the heat from plasma rounds zipping past or the added dust and debris kicked up by missed shots—they ran about forty yards before darting behind a large pile of stones and bricks. Korso leaned around the pile, shooting a soldier in the chest while Von caught a second in the throat.

"That was mean." Korso drew his second pistol, coercing their pursuers to slow their advance. "And since I got you all to myself, why don't we talk about you and my sister."

"This is hardly the time for a declaration of intentions." Von pivoted to his left, firing at another wave of soldiers.

Korso ducked back behind the pile of debris, coughing as a cloud of dust filled his lungs. "So you have intentions?"

"Now isn't the time."

"I disagree."

"I can't see how you can joke at a time like this," Von replied, firing at another soldier.

"Actually, this brings back memories." Korso tapped Von's shoulder, pointing towards a narrow street between two standing buildings. Waiting for his nod of understanding, Korso fired a long string of covering fire as Von ran into the alley before covering Korso.

Sprinting through the varied curves of the alley, the duo veered into what looked like an old diner, pausing only to shoot back when needed, before emerging back into the open. Racing down another road, they slid into an old Hestron trench, narrowly avoiding a storm of orange plasma. Korso turned to fire at their pursuers when he spotted an old fuel cell and hurried over to see if it still had any power.

"What are you doing?" Von ducked, staring at Korso.

"I got an idea." Korso grabbed the cell with a smirk, sliding a pistol back in its holster. "You're a good shot right?"

"I am."

"As they pour through the door, I'll toss this over and you shoot it."

"Why?"

"You shoot, it explodes, they die." Korso waited as the soldiers started to emerge from the diner before heaving the fuel cell over their heads. An instant before it hit one of the soldiers in the head, Von fired, causing it to explode, killing the group in the doorway and bringing the dilapidated remains of the diner down on top of the rest. "See?"

"An interesting trick."

"Just something I picked up during the war. Now let's get going before more show up."

Korso and Von sprinted their way through the city, avoiding EDM soldiers as best they could until they reached the transport and found Rachael, Orrin, and Lizabeth waiting for them.

"You two took your time," Rachael exclaimed, mirroring Korso's relief, as she and Lizabeth jumped in the front with Orrin, who was already starting the vehicle.

"I stopped to watch a bana dance," Korso replied with a playful smirk while he and Von jumped in the back an instant before Orrin pulled off. Eager to get out of the city, he looked over to Lizabeth, flashing her a reassuring smile. "Still glad you tagged along?"

"At least this is better than that time you found that pijak cave," Lizabeth replied, pushing aside the fear he knew she must have felt.

Von finished his exchange with Orrin and leaned back, looking angrier than usual. "Korso, you said you had an army hidden somewhere."

"I said I had a couple of platoons," Korso corrected.

"And weapons? We will need all the weapons we can muster, if we are to move against Cole."

"I got all the weapons you need on Resoe Faest."

"Lord Von," Orrin interrupted. "All of our forces are ready to leave as soon as we arrive."

"Tell them to go now," Von ordered. "Have them hide behind the moons until we arrive."

"Does anyone else hear that?" Rachael twisted in her seat, peering around.

"I don't hear anything?" Orrin veered the transport around a large pile of debris.

Korso started to respond when he noticed a distinct rumbling and joined Rachael in her search. Catching sight of a large shadow moving between a pair of buildings and a fresh cloud of dirt too big to attribute to the wind, he held one of his pistols at the ready, hopping he was imagining the growing hum in his ears. "Hey Orrin, faster might better right now."

The sound of cracking stone pulled Korso's attention back to the rear left in time to see a twelve meter long sand colored wedge smash through a building wall and onto the street behind them.

"What is that?" Lizabeth asked, panic lining her voice.

"That…" Korso winced, staring at the large turret in the wedges center and the two smaller ones positioned on either side. "That would be a mark two delta tank."

"Can we out run it?" Rachael asked.

"We got a choice?" Korso replied over the howling wind, turning to fire, not that it would do much good.

Von twisted in his seat, firing a volley of rounds at the glowing oval disks beneath the tank whenever an opportunity presented itself. "Aim for the repulser lifts."

"They're shielded." Korso glanced at Von.

"Against heavy weapon fire," Von replied between shots. "I've spent enough time dealing with them to know they have flaws."

"Hang on!" Orrin swerved wide to the left, just in time to avoid an ion blast from the tanks main gun.

Ears ringing from the following blast, Korso released his grip on the transports seat and resumed firing. "Do tell."

"The shields don't activate from small arms fire. If we shoot out enough of the lifts, it goes down," Von yelled over the continuous ion fire bombarding them with bursts of super-heated air and dirt.

"Oh… well it's new." Korso pressed himself down in the seat, ducking as a large rock kicked up by the tank whizzed past his head. "Of course, if they don't climb to kill us from above, that bit of intel isn't going to help much."

"Not to be the downer in the group, but it's getting closer," Lizabeth stated.

Struggling to shoot and not get flung from the swerving vehicle, Korso swallowed, refusing to let his apprehension take root and picked his shots, firing every time the tank bounced high enough to shoot at a repulser lift. Wishing he had a pair goggles to protect his vision from the clouds of dirt stinging his eyes as they sped out of the city, he caught the sound of Rachael's voice and turned to find her holding her comm.

"Orrin." Von grabbed onto the door of the transport an instant before the T'loak soldier jerked the controls to left.

Crying out in surprise, Korso slammed into Von before getting flung into the opposite door. "A little warning next time?"

"Hang on," Rachael shouted over another burst of ion fire that rocked the transport, kicking up chunks of rock and dirt.

Orrin twisted the controls, banking wide to the right and gunned it, leaving Korso confused about the sudden shift in direction when the sound of a much larger engine caught his attention. Looking back towards the tank—which was just starting to match their maneuver—Korso felt a relieved smile as the *Sprinthawk* soared overhead and fired a pair of concussion missiles. Not designed to withstand warship munitions, the tank exploded in a brilliant flash of orange and yellow. Rachael and Lizabeth let out an overjoyed cheer even as the shockwave almost tipped over the transport.

"Perfect shooting," Rachael spoke into her comm.

Sliding his pistol into its holster, Korso leaned over the front seat and grabbed Rachael's hand, lifting her comm to talk. "Dee, I could kiss you right now."

"You're welcome," Dee replied over the comm. "The T'loak fleet is ready to go, but Chaple's forces are already moving towards us."

"Then pick us up and lets bolt," Korso ordered.

"Roger that."

Korso released Rachael's hand and flashed a smirk. "Calling in an airstrike, not bad for a brat with no combat experience."

"Still glad you let me tag along?" Rachael smiled. "Jerk."

"More and more." Korso watched his ship land ahead of them while Orrin pulled to a stop. Vaulting out of the transport, he let Rachael and the others run up the descending boarding ramp first before slapping the control to seal the hatch and sprinted to the bridge.

"Why is it every time we go someplace, someone is either trying to kill you or chase you off world?" Dee asked, pulling back on the controls and flying off.

"It's not my fault." Korso sat in the co-pilots seat, powering up weapons and preparing a set of coordinates for the rest of Von's people. "Besides, this time they weren't after me or Rachael."

"I see." Dee laughed while Lizabeth took Von and Orrin to the back and strapped in. "And I see Lizabeth is back…and with Prince Von."

"Don't get me started on that." Korso finished sending their destination to the T'loak ships and reached for the fold controls. "You did finish fixing the fold-generator, right?"

"I did."

"Then we are out of here." Korso breathed a sigh of relief as he activated the fold-generator, elated to be leaving Farina far, far behind him.

* * *

Chaple stood on the bridge of the *Black Bell* and watched as the last of the T'loak ships slipped into hyperspace. Frustrated that Von and the Princess had both escaped him, he was more disappointed that he would not be presenting them both to Cole as a gift, but patience was always one of his best qualities. For now, he would simply have to continue his hunt, a game he enjoyed more than making the kill, and wait.

"Re-call all fighters and begin tracking the *Sprinthawk* at once." Chaple turned on his heel and started towards his office in the back of the bridge.

"Yes sir."

Chaple stepped through the metallic sliding doors and called for the lights as the door closed. Walking past his diligently maintained desk, he stepped onto a circular holopad and reached over to the control panel on his left, initiating a comm channel to the Imperial Palace. "Lord Cole." He bowed as an image of Cole flicked into existence.

"Chaple, how goes the hunt for our favorite bastard Prince?" Cole asked, a hint of irritation lining his voice.

"Unfortunately, I bring ill tidings. I had laid a trap for Von in what was left of Adom City, but he and his fleet eluded capture."

"So he is still alive?" Cole narrowed his eyes.

"Yes. I did not anticipate Korso and Princess Rachael's interference."

"Korso was on Farina?" Cole paused, crossing his arms, the anger disappearing from his voice. "That means Korso has his sister."

"Sister?" Chaple felt his eyebrows rise.

"The woman who was being delivered to you was Lizabeth Korso." Cole smiled. "If she is with him, then he must know that I'm looking for his hidden base, and so he'll want to beat me to it."

"I have begun tracking his ship but…"

"I know the planet and the general area he is heading, but not the exact location. Go to Resoe Faest in the Azulan system, the Crimson Knights will be there when you arrive. Korso will take his time getting there—he'll need to be sure he's lost you first—so you should be able to beat him there."

"What of the base, when it's found?"

"Take anything of interest then destroy it."

"As you command, my Lord," Chaple replied with a bow. A second later the image of Cole disappeared and Chaple stepped off of the pad and marched back on to the bridge.

Patience was the key to any successful hunt, and preparation the key for the kill. He wielded both with the proficiency of a sparrow in flight, and was once again looking forward to presenting the heads of his prey to his Emperor.

CHAPTER NINE

Korso sat staring at the waves of bluish light that washed over the *Sprinthawk's* hull as they flew through hyperspace. After spending the better part of two days jumping from one system to next in order to avoid any tracking programs Chaple may have employed, he was glad to be on his way to the Azulan system, if only to end Von's constant pestering. Turning his chair towards the entrance, Korso caught the sound of Orrin talking with Rachael and Lizabeth in the galley—and he'd have sworn he could hear Von scowling—as Dee walked in and sat in the co-pilots chair.

"Am I disturbing you?" Dee asked.

"Just wondering how we became a royal transport." Korso spun his chair to face Dee. "Or how things might have been different if we had gone down a different hallway."

"Do you regret choosing to help Princess Rachael?"

"Nah. Who cares if I've been branded a traitor and my oldest friend wants me dead." Korso forced a laugh, knowing Dee would never buy it. "And to be honest, I'm kinda starting to like having her around."

"I didn't notice." Dee let out an amused chuckle and glanced towards the galley. "I believe the two of you are good for each other, complimentary."

"Do I detect a note of sarcasm?"

"Not at all. The two of you are a prime example of a souls recognition of its counter point in another."

"Never pegged you as the romantic type," Korso replied, off put by the comment. "And you've been talking with Liz, haven't you?"

"Maybe." Dee flashed a sly smirk. "She seems quite taken with our princely T'loak."

Korso glared at Dee for a long moment before he was unable to keep from laughing. "You're enjoying all this way too much."

"I take the shots presented to me." Dee leaned back and gazed out the forward view port for a few minutes before looking back to Korso. "Eventually, we are going to have to confront Cole."

"I know."

"What do you intend to do?"

Korso leaned back, returning his chair to its forward position and let out a somber breath. "For whatever reason, the guy I grew up with is gone. So I'm left with one option. I have to kill him."

"It doesn't have to be you."

"Doesn't it?" Korso spun towards Dee. "Rachael can't, Von shouldn't, and I won't shove this off on you. It has to be me. I'm the Seraph Prime, and he was my friend. It has to be me." Korso sat motionless, allowing himself to remember running around with Cole as he returned his gaze to the forward viewport, when a soft buzzing sound yanked him back to reality. Peering down at the console, he let out a tired breath and stood. "We're coming up on Resoe Faest."

Pushing aside his memories, Korso made his way towards the galley but paused in the archway spotting Rachael sitting on the table talking to Orrin and Lizabeth, the latter of whom was sitting far too close to Von for his liking. Growing more and more curious about what had happened between his sister and Von, Korso stepped into the room just as Rachael and Lizabeth burst into laughter. "What?"

"Nothing," Lizabeth responded, trying to suppress a giggle.

"What did you tell her?"

Lizabeth shrugged. "I just told her about that time you found that large bird and tried to feed it a rock."

"And how you tried to bash its head in when it wouldn't eat it." Rachael laughed.

"Okay…" Korso let out an annoyed groan and leaned over Lizabeth, adding an air of menace to his voice. "Liz, new rule: no more stories about our childhood; or should I share the one about the goney bogi cave?"

"You wouldn't?" Lizabeth's face turned bright red as everyone looked towards her.

"I would."

"This I have to hear." Rachael turned back towards Korso."

"I'm a little curious myself," Von stated, cracking the slightest semblance of a smile Korso had seen from the man since they had met.

Korso put on a malicious grin, enjoying the look of embarrassment Lizabeth wore. "Well, this one morning when we were kids, Liz comes running into…

Lizabeth jumped to her feet, covering Korso's mouth with her hand. "I'll behave."

"Good. Now, we're about to hit Resoe Faest." Korso felt a slight shift in the ships gravity, indicating that they had just dropped out of hyperspace, and motioned for everyone to follow.

Stepping back into the cockpit, Korso found that Dee had joined Von's fleet behind a large gas giant on the edge of the system.

"Why are we way out here?" Orrin asked.

"Sensors picked up some comm chatter coming from Resoe Faest as we exited hyperspace," Dee responded.

Korso stepped over to the main console. "From who?"

Dee leaned back. "It appears that the Crimson Knights have beaten us here."

"I thought this place was secret?" Rachael glanced at Korso.

"So did I." Korso swore under his breath, wishing for once in his life Cole wasn't so adept at predicting his opponents move.

Rachael stepped over to Korso's side. "Well, if the Knights are here then so is Chaple."

"So… shouldn't we leave before they find us?" Lizabeth asked from the back of the group.

"That's not an option," Von stated, shaking his head. "We need weapons and reinforcements if we are to win this war."

"Agreed, and we should be safe here for a while, so long as they don't look too closely." Korso turned to face the group. "The real problem is getting off the planet unnoticed with everything we came for."

"And how will you do that?" Von asked.

"I have no idea." Korso smirked. "Dee, you stay here with Lizabeth and keep an eye on the Knights and Von's fleet. Maybe see if you can give us a heads up when Chaple arrives, but stay out of sight. I'll take the rest planet side in the shuttle. We should be able to land undetected and find Webber."

"Understood." Dee nodded.

"Be careful." Lizabeth squeezed Von's hand as he and Orrin stepped past.

"Don't worry about me," Korso teased, allowing himself to be pushed along by Rachael. Making their way down to the cargo hold and into the shuttle, Korso powered it up and waited for everyone to climb in.

"So how are we going to get past the Knight's scanners?" Rachael asked.

Throttling up the repulser lifts, Korso flew the shuttle out of the hold, accelerating towards the fifth planet in the system and brought up a small holographic image of Resoe Faest. "Comm signals from the Knights puts them up here." He pointed towards a blinking red marker, then to a blue one. "The base is down there. If we come in from the southern hemisphere, they probably won't detect us."

"Probably?" Von repeated, his tone dubious.

"Don't worry." Rachael smirked and looked over her shoulder. "He's upgraded. It's a stealthy flying bucket."

"This is your Captain speaking; please return all mouths to their full shut up position." Korso returned her smirk, before banking around the first of several moons.

"So Ethrians are this chatty and this isn't some new form of torture." Von leaned back in his seat.

Resisting the urge to harass him further, Korso focused on the sensor board, searching for any sign that they might have been detected as they flew through the planet's atmosphere. Still keeping an eye on the sensors, he dropped the shuttle down to tree level and began searching for a suitable place to land within the lush forest that surrounded the area. Spotting an opening, he dipped below the tree tops and tucked the shuttle between a pair of large trees.

"How far are we from your base?" Von asked while everyone started to climb out in the shade provided by the thick canopy of teal and green leaves.

"About two miles to the east." Korso used the shuttle remote to scan a nearby bush before camouflaging the shuttle.

"You couldn't find a closer spot to land?" Rachael shot Korso an annoyed look while checking her pistol.

"It's better that he didn't, Princess." Orrin handed Von a rifle before slinging his own over his shoulder and started after Von. "It makes it harder for our enemies to track us."

They walked in silence, navigating through the thick foliage as best they could, for ten minutes when Korso noticed Rachael staring at him. "What?"

"I was just wondering what you're gonna do when this is all over?" Rachael stepped around a thick tree and returned her gaze towards him. "After I get my throne and Von can go home, what happens to you?"

"Why? You getting tired of my playful charm?"

"As much as pains me to admit, I've grown to appreciate your juvenile ways."

"Really?" Korso ducked under a low branch with a smile. "I might have been convinced to stick around, but you're just too mean. Always calling me names, making fun of my shuttle, and the obscene language…"

“Shut up.” Rachael laughed, pushing him into a tree.

Korso grinned, over exaggerating his impact with the tree. “See?”

“Princess.” Orrin stopped a few yards behind the pair of Ethrians.

Rachael turned to face him, letting her smile fade. “What is it?”

“We are not alone.” Von raised his pulse rifle and scanned the surrounding tree line. Stepping closer to Von and Orrin, Korso reached for one of his pistols a moment before twenty soldiers in blue and black combat gear stepped out from behind the trees. “Who are you?”

“Sergeant Anton Webber, acting commander of the Band of the Hawk.” He motioned for the other soldiers to lower their weapons and stepped over to Korso with a salute. “I was startin’ to think you wouldn’t make it sir.”

“We had a few hitches along the way.” Korso returned the salute.

“Princess,” Webber said with a bow. “If I may ask, why are the T’loak here?”

“They’re our new allies,” Korso responded.

“Ah.” Webber offered Von a hesitant bow. “Prince Von, Princess Rachael, and all, welcome to what we have come to name the sea of trees. However, we really should get inside; the Crimson Knights have patrols searching the entire area.”

* * *

Lira stood in the control room of an old but well maintained base and observed the Crimson Knights scurrying about the climate controlled room like insects. Elated with the fact that she was given command of the Knights, she suppressed a smirk, reveling in the enjoyment of watching her orders being carried out. An enjoyment she planned to savor far more than her predecessor.

Noticing the saluting Knight that had stepped over to her side, Lira waited for a long minute before acknowledging him. "What is it?"

"Ma'am, the *Black Bell* has just landed outside the northern gate."

"Inform them that I will meet them there." Lira turned on her heel and marched out of the room, keeping her pace brisk. Striding through the dull colored corridors, she began to wonder what would bring the Emperor's favorite assassin into her assignment, but elected to let the question fade when she found him and an EDM soldier walking towards her.

"Lieutenant, Where is Vega?" Chaple stopped in front of her.

"It's *Captain* now, sir, and the *late* Captain Vega was relieved of his command." Lira let a hint of pride sneak into her voice. "I am now in command of the Crimson Knights."

"I see. Have you located the Princess or Korso's hidden compound?"

"Not as yet, but I have narrowed down the possible location to a few thousand kilometers of our position and have men systematically scanning the surrounding forest."

"Then redouble your efforts," Chaple ordered, ice lining every word. "And begin jamming all comm traffic coming to or leaving the planet. I doubt Korso and Von could have landed their small fleet without your notice, and since I detected no sign of them when I arrived, they must be hiding somewhere outside the system."

"That makes finding them quite the task."

"I don't want them found. I want Korso cut off from escape and allies."

"With all due respect, this is my command." Lira shot Chaple an irritated glare. "The EDM has no authority here."

"My orders are from Lord Cole, and if you are questioning him, then I kill you here and now." Chaple paused matching her glare with a disturbing, placid expression, despite the menacing tone in his voice. "Now, I am taking command here and you will do as I have instructed, understood?"

"Yes sir." Lira forced a begrudging salute, biting back a flood of anger. "But how does all this help find the base or the Princess?"

"As I've said, I'm not going to look for Korso or the Princess." Chaple shrugged, stepping past her. "A good hunter creates a scenario where the prey is forced to come to him."

* * *

"This is crazy, even for you," Rachael stated, staring at the floating image of their home system in the darkened conference room of the compound Korso had built years ago.

"I agree." Von leaned on a small silver table, wearing a discouraged look on his face. "Our best option for reaching Ethria is to pass through the Zol Mists and attack from there."

"It's how the T'loak would attack," Orrin added.

Korso shook his head and glanced at everyone gathered around the oval table. "You're thinking too traditional. Cole isn't the head of the Ethrian Defense Ministry by accident. He's very, *very*, good at his job and he's turned Ethria into one of the most heavily fortified planets in the quadrant. Trust me when I say he's already thought of every logical attack the T'loak might have thought up. And Ethrian SOP on planetary assaults are just as useless."

"Still, your plan seems a bit… dangerous," Rachael responded.

"We don't have the manpower to slug it out with Cole, and even if we did, we end up killing a lot of innocent soldiers." Korso tapped a switch on the control panel and deactivated the hologram. "My plan minimizes the potential casualties, is doable with what we have, and has the benefit of having never been tried before."

Von offered a thoughtful nod. "And you believe this can get you to the imperial palace?"

"Absolutely, sir." Webber stepped over to the table. "Put the Hawks behind the controls of a fighter and we'll thread needles for you."

"Alright, so we actually have a plan for once." Rachael nodded in agreement. "Now how are we gonna get off the planet with the Crimson Knights watching anything that moves?"

"Been thinking about that." Korso adjusted the florescent lights back to normal. "Since the Knights are all docked at the old base, we just gotta put a land-lock on them."

"Land-lock?" Rachael shook her head, confused.

"It was a program designed to stop enemy ships from leaving if they ever breached the base," Webber explained. "This was a key position to hold during the war and we kept a lot of important Intel here."

"And, we were constantly fighting off enemy raids," Korso added. "So we needed a way stop anyone from escaping with anything important."

"But how would we get into the base to use it?" Orrin inquired.

"We walk," Korso replied plainly.

"Oh yeah, I'm sure they'll just let us stroll right in." Rachael leaned against the table and starred at Korso.

"Princess, I believe he means through the service tunnel that connects this base to the old one," Webber explained.

Rachael arched an eyebrow. "What tunnel?"

"When I built this place, I made sure there was a way to get from here to there unnoticed." Korso smiled and leaned close to her. "And it's obviously still a secret since the Crimson Knights haven't kicked in the door yet."

Rachael replied with a roll of her eyes and pushed him back. "Since you have it all figured out, what are we waiting for?"

Korso turned towards Webber. "How long until the Hawks and Raiders are ready to fly?"

"I'll have them ready within an hour," Webber replied.

"You got half that. I'll get the code input at the old base. Just be ready to fly when I comm. It won't take them long to get an override code from Cole."

"Yes sir." Webber saluted before stepping over to another soldier.

"Shouldn't take me more than forty minutes to get there and back." Korso started towards the oval doorway but stopped when Rachael grabbed his arm.

"You can't go alone."

"She's right," Von said. "You may need help… should things go sideways."

"If you insist." Korso relented with a smirk and started towards the lift that would take them to the storage level and service tunnel.

* * *

Driving an old maintenance cart through the four kilometer tunnel, with only the dull orange emergency lights to guide him, Korso pulled to a stop in front of a large freight lift. Climbing out with the others, he stepped over to the right, running both hands over the grimy wall.

"Will the lift get us to wherever we need to go?" Orrin stopped in front of the lift and looked back along with Von.

"It'll get us inside," Korso replied, keeping his hands on the wall while moving towards the lift. "But I don't want to power it up and clue anyone in to our presence."

"So what are you doing?" Rachael asked.

"Fondling the wall." Korso smirked as his fingers dragged across a metal covering. Sliding the cover open with one hand, he grabbed the small lever and turned it to the right, causing a two foot wide door to pop open with a clunk. "After you, oh doubting one."

Rachael groaned in annoyance, waving her hand at the cloud of dust. "Do you always have to be such a smartass?"

"Yeah, pretty much." Korso stepped through the opening and gazed up the narrow shaft, grateful that the few lights that were installed still worked, and started to climb the ladder. "You always have to make snide comments?"

"Yeah, pretty much," Rachael replied, following along with the others.

"How far up do we have to climb?" Von inquired from the rear of the group.

"This'll take us as far as the sub-level storage room." Korso continued to climb; wishing the stagnant air in the shaft had better circulation.

"And where do we initiate the land-lock?"

"Best spot would be the main control room, but, gotta figure the Crimson Banas have already set up shop there. So we'll have to get to the secondary control. I should be able to lock them out of the computers from there."

Reaching the top, Korso stepped over to the door at the end of the short corridor and pulled it open, relishing the rush of fresh cycled air. Wincing for a moment as his eyes adjusted to the florescent lighting, he scanned the large barren room before moving inside and over to a much larger door.

Satisfied that the corridor was clear, Korso lead them through the facility, ducking behind pillars or into empty rooms whenever any Knights passed by. Finding their way to the western wing, the sound of voices echoing through the corridor ahead caused them to pause. Korso reached for his right pistol out of reflex and pressed his back against a cream colored wall, peering around the corner to find a pair of soldiers in EDM uniforms conversing.

Korso caught a nod from Von and cautiously followed him around the corner. Sneaking over to the first soldier, Korso whipped the butt of his pistol into the back of the soldier's head, while Von grabbed the second's shoulder, spun him around and punched him in the throat before shoving him head first into the wall.

Korso kicked the first soldier on the head, knocking him out, and glanced over towards Von. "That was mean."

"I should have shot him," Von replied, his voice dry. "But your sister and Orrin have requested I try a softer approach."

Rachael followed Orrin over and looked down at the two soldiers. "I guess Chaple finally got here."

"So why didn't we know about it?" Von turned towards Korso.

"Good question." Korso pulled his comm out, trying to stifle his growing apprehension while attempting to reach Dee. "Long range signals not getting through."

"Then Chaple may have already taken our ships," Von stated.

"Or might be trying to cut us off from them," Orrin replied.

Rachael looked from Von to Korso. "Either way, it sounds like a trap. So what do we do?"

"Stick to the plan. It's all we can do right now." Korso pointed to an open door a few feet away. "The secondary control room is there. Let's get in and get out before someone misses these two."

Korso hurried over to the control room, peaking inside before stepping into the windowless chamber, and powered up the center computer terminal as he sat. "See if you can find the source of the jamming signal."

"Right," Orrin replied, moving over to a station on the left side of room.

"How long will it take?" Rachael stood next him.

"Not long, but the computer isn't registering the *Black Bell* in the dock or hanger bay." Korso finished programing the computer to target all ships within the base and waited to execute the command. "Find it?"

Orrin shook his head. "It's not coming from here. My guess is it's coming from Chaple's ship."

"Figures. I guess we comm Dee after we get off world." Korso tapped the final key to initiate the land-lock program. "Time to go. They'll know we're here as soon as someone tries to fly off."

Hurrying out of the small room, Korso followed everyone back into the corridor, and was surprised to find group of Crimson Knights heading their way.

"Don't move," one of the Knights yelled, raising his rifle, only to get shot by Von while Orrin shot another. Whipping out his own pistol, Korso unloaded a volley of plasma rounds at the remaining Knights as they ducked behind the corner.

"Control, enemy contact, west wing," another Knight shouted.

"Just once I'd like to get in and out as planned," Korso exclaimed, continuing to fire.

"What now?" Rachael asked.

"We take the long way around." Korso grabbed Rachael and pushed her towards the opposite end of the corridor before sprinting after her. Pausing where the hall forked in two, he fired another long barrage to cover Von and Orrin as they followed.

The sound of the perusing Knight's boots hitting the tiled floor managed to reach Korso's ears even over the blaring alarms and bursts of plasma fire as they raced through the cream paneled corridors.

"Down here." Korso Motioned towards the upcoming stairwell while retrieving a grenade from his belt and throwing it at the perusing Knights. Feeling the heat as the grenade exploded behind them, he darted into the stairwell and found his partners shooting at a squad of Chaple's goons who were trying to advance towards them.

Korso cursed—jumping back to avoid getting his head blasted off—and returned fire, catching one of the soldiers in the chest. Leaning over the rail, Von shot another Knight while Orrin and Rachael took out the last two.

Continuing down the stairs until they reached the floor they wanted, they cautiously scanned the corridor before resuming their sprint. Korso rounded a corner, surprised by the lack of waiting troops considering that the Knights or Chaple had to be using the internal sensors to follow their movements, and began to ponder why when a flashing yellow light ahead answered his question.

"They're trying to seal us in." Korso pushed himself to run faster, darting under the first of descending blast doors.

Spotting the storage room they had used earlier, Korso ran beneath a second blast door and turned just as Von ducked through. Panic freezing his veins, Korso saw Rachael and Orrin attempt to slide under the transparent door only to bounce off with a sickening thud an instant after it slammed shut, trapping them on the other side.

"Rachael!" Korso darted over to the wall terminal and typing in his override code.

"Get them out," Von exclaimed.

"I'm trying," Korso growled, while the computer rejected his access code.

Korso tried again, but as he did, the door behind Rachael and Orrin opened and Chaple strode into the corridor followed by Lira and a dozen soldiers. Twisting with his rifle ready, Orrin fired into the group—nailing two of the soldiers—but Lira reacted quickly, ducking low while unloading a plasma round that caught him in the shoulder.

"Orrin!" Von slammed into the blast door, helpless to do anything but watch as Orrin dropped his rifle and fall back into the door. Rachael tried to draw her sword but was grabbed by a group of Knights and dragged over to Lira.

"Let her go." Orrin forced himself to stand—leaving a large streak of blood on the door as he did—extending his sword while drawing it and slashed one of the Knights across the face. Staggering forward, he parried a strike from a soldier and caught him with a slash to the chest, but was rewarded with a shot to the leg.

"Orrin." Rachael struggled to free herself as Orrin fell to the floor.

Chaple sauntered towards Orrin wearing an unnerving, predatory smile. “A heroic effort. As to be expected from the T’loak, but in vain.” Pulling a long, slender dagger from his sleeve, he rolled a gasping Orrin to his back and peered over to Von.

“You’re after me, let him go,” Von demanded, his eyes wide and unblinking.

“I had hopped this would be you.” Chaple pushed the dagger through the bottom of Orrin’s jaw—smiling through every pained gurgle the fallen warrior made—and continued until the blade disappeared into Orrin’s skull. Keeping his eye’s locked on Von, he twisted the dagger before yanking it free.

Von howled; fury and sorrow pouring out of him as he smashed his fist against the blast door.

“I look forward to killing you in a similar manner.” Chaple shifted his gaze over to Korso. “I will be returning to Ethria. If you wish to reclaim the Princess, I shall await you along with Lord Cole, should you manage an escape.”

“Like hell.” Overwhelmed with horror, Korso aimed and fired at Chaple, barely aware of his own movements or the sound of the rounds ricocheting off the shielded glass. Refusing to give up, he moved back to the control panel while Chaple and Lira dragged Rachael off.

“Take them,” Lira ordered.

“We need to move.” Von turned and started towards the storage room.

“I’m not leaving her.” Korso continued punching keys on the terminal, trying every code he ever knew.

“If we stay, we die.” Von stepped over and ripped him away from the panel. “Live today, and fight tomorrow.”

Korso glanced over to the soldiers preparing to open the blast door and forced himself to turn away, hating that he knew Von was right.

Following Von through the storage room door and into the hidden shaft, Korso sealed the door behind them and pulled out his comm. "Webber?"

"Sir?"

"Get going, now. Link up with Dee and the T'loak at the rendezvous coordinates. We'll catch up in the shuttle."

"Yes sir," Webber responded.

Sliding down the ladder faster than he should have, Korso bolted towards the maintenance cart, barely giving Von time to jump in before peeling off. He mashed the accelerator forward, growing more and more frustrated by the carts limited speed and found himself repeating the same thought over again. He needed to get to his ship. He needed to get to Ethria. He needed to get to Rachael.

CHAPTER TEN

Cole stood in front of a large glass window in the palace throne room and stared over the city sitting a few miles away under the afternoon sun. He began to wonder if any of the people wandering about his city knew the tireless effort he put into preserving their blissful, ignorant way of life. He had little doubt that history would one day label him a tyrant, but he would be a tyrant that preserved the Empire. He could live with that.

The only real obstacle left between him and the achievement of his goals was an old friend who refused to die and the branz he protected. But they would be dealt with like everything else that has ever stood in his way. They would die for the good of the realm, and he would do what he was born to do. Protect the Empire.

Noticing the approach of a guard in the windows reflection, Cole peered over his shoulder. “What is it?”

“My Lord, Chaple and Captain Lira have just landed and wish to speak with you. Also, Chaple says he brings a royal gift.”

Dismissing the guard with a nod, Cole continued to gaze out the window, mulling over what Chaple had meant. In their last communication, Chaple had said that he killed one Von’s top Lieutenants, and that he had left most of the Crimson Knights to salvage Korso’s underground base. Dismissing his thoughts, he turned towards the entrance, catching the sound of approaching footsteps, and saw Chaple striding in. “I don’t suppose you’ve come to tell me Korso is dead?”

“Regrettably no, however, I brought a gift to honor you as penance for that failure.” Chaple motioned towards the door as Lira hauled Rachael in, her hands bound in front of her.

Unable to hide his delight, Cole laughed while Rachael struggled to free herself from Lira’s grasp, and stepped over as if she were an old squad mate. “Princess, it’s so lovely to have you back home." Enjoying the look of disdain on her face, he stepped back. "Isn't it customary to kneel before your Emperor?"

"Since you murdered my father, *I'm* the Empress, and you should kneel to me!" Rachael yanked her arm free from Lira.

"Still just as petulant as ever, or is that because you think Korso can save you?"

"He'll come for me. The only question is will he kill you before I do."

"I'm sure he'll try. He and the T'loak will try to smash their way past the outer defenses and attack the planet head on because it's so obvious a tactic that no one but him would try something so insane. So I'll allow them their all or nothing gambit, and once they're committed, my Dreadnaughts will swoop in from outside the system and remove them from my skies. Korso will never set foot on this planet again." Cole moved over to Lira, taking Rachael's sword from her and thumbing the blades release. "Captain, remove her restraints then you can leave. Chaple, go and make sure everything is ready for Korso when he arrives."

"As you wish my Lord." Chaple bowed then followed Lira out.

"This is a splendid sword." Twirling the weapon around him, Cole brought the blade to eye level admiring the craftsmanship for a moment before tossing it at Rachael's feet.

"What are you doing?" Rachael gave him a skeptical glance.

"I've heard that you were tutored by one of the better swordsmen on the planet, and I'm sure you're aware that dueling is bit of a hobby of mine. So, since we have a little time before Korso arrives, I'll have to entertain myself by playing with you." Cole smiled and drew his own sword. "You just said you wanted to kill me, and I would hate to kill you and leave you filled with regrets. Here's your chance."

"Not afraid I'll cut your tutin head off?" Rachael reached down and picked up her sword, her eyes locked on his and narrowed in fury.

"Not in the least. As I've said, I'm fairly gifted with a sword. I once entered the planet wide swordsman tournament with Korso a while back."

"I heard Korso made it to the finals."

"Korso had little formal training, but he is still the best swordsman I've come across. He truly earned his spot in second place." Cole smiled, remembering the excitement he shared with Korso, and the rush as the crowd cheered. "But I took first."

Rachael lunged forward with a series of fluid strikes, hatred fueling her assault. Swaying around or parrying most of her attacks, Cole couldn't help but admire the gracefulness of her movements, despite her anger. *She's competent, albeit predictable, and her anger makes her sloppy. Still, at least she's willing to fight, unlike her father.*

Stepping back to avoid a downward slash, Cole was caught by surprise as Rachael spun on her heel, landing a solid kick to his jaw. Instinct taking over, he deflected her following attack and pivoted to her left, driving an elbow into the side of her head. Catching her across the chin with a punch as she staggered back, he lashed out with his sword, mindful of the force he used to insure that the wound he placed on her arm was superficial.

"You really are talented with a blade." Cole massaged his lower lip and smirked, surprised to find blood on his fingers. "But you'll need to do better if you intend to avoid your father's fate."

Rachael snarled, lunging at him again, but Cole stepped into her attack, locking her arms to keep her close.

"It really doesn't have to be like this," Cole continued. "A public display of your blessing would go a long way to way in solidifying my rule. Kneel before your Emperor and, in the end, I promise you a dignified exile."

"I'd rather die first."

"That is the other option." Cole pushed her back. "This all ends the same; you just lack the foresight to realize it. You are going to die, Korso will die, and I will be the one that saves the Empire from crumbling beneath the heel of our enemies."

Cole loosed a kick to her hand, knocking her sword free before grabbing a hand full of her hair, and flung her to the ground. Standing over Rachael, savoring the fear he saw in her eyes, Cole noticed some movement near the entrance and looked over to find the guard. "What now?"

"We just received a report stating that a fleet of T'loak frigates is in route to the system. ETA, thirty minutes," the guard replied.

"What perfect timing." Cole motioned for the soldier to leave and looked down at Rachael. "It is so gratifying when people behave exactly as I predict."

"I hope Korso kills you." Rachael glared at him, loathing twisting her pretty face. "Because if he doesn't, I'll make sure your death lasts for days."

"And yet, I'm the tyrant." Cole laughed, eager for his reunion with Korso. "You, like Korso, are far too emotional. He'll take one look at your battered face and play right into my hands."

"That was the point of this?"

"Of course." Cole regarded her for a long moment, surprised by her bewilderment. "I am not a monster. Well… I am, but I am also a patriot, one with vision enough to see the coming disaster looming on our doorstep if we don't prepare."

"The only enemies facing the Empire are the ones you made," Rachael spat.

"You're as short sided as your father, but you won't live long enough for me to say I told you so."

* * *

"We are approaching Ethria now," Dee stated over the sound of ion fire hammering the *Sprinthawk's* shields. "And Cole knows we're here. As plans go, this is probably one of the more irrational ones you've come up with."

"I was never overly fond of conventional." Korso looked away from the hulking masses floating around him to the screen on the center console. The wedge of blue dots representing his allies began to break into smaller clusters, meeting heavy resistance from the planetary defense forces highlighted in red. "You can always bug out."

"And miss being a part of the latest Korso story…" Dee grunted as another blast rocked the *Sprinthawk*. "Still wish I was flying with you though."

Korso laughed, looking over to the seat next to him where Von sat. "I need you there. The *Sprinthawk* has to be leading the pack if we want Cole to go for it."

Returning his attention to his own task, Korso veered the shuttle around a large asteroid and checked the position of the Hawk's fighters as they weaved their way through the asteroid belt on the opposite side of Ethria.

His plan was simple enough, provided he could survive the dense field of rock long enough to reach his target. Distract Cole with a frontal assault that he would assume was real while Korso led multiple squads of fighters and four troop transports around the far side of planet. It was a tried and true flanking maneuver, one Cole would never expect from him.

"If things go sideways, watch out for Liz." Korso pushed the image of his sister crying on the T'loak ship they had left her on from his mind and glanced at Von. "Don't suppose you have something to add?"

"No." Von shook his head. "I intend to live."

"Good hunting," Dee replied.

"Back at you." Switching the comm channel to the fighters, Korso took a breath, preparing to accelerate towards the planet. "All wings, go when ready."

"Copy that," Webber's voice replied.

Watching while the fighters shot passed his shuttle—on their way to harass potential reinforcements and clear a landing zone for the ground forces—Korso jammed the throttle forward, speeding out of the asteroid belt. Breaking through the atmosphere, he banked right, leaving the approaching enemy fighters to the Hawks, and headed straight for the palace.

The Emerald Raiders poured out of the transports below, exchanging fire in the open courtyards, while Korso landed in one of the gardens. Stepping onto the plush grass, Korso ducked behind a low stone wall, drawing his pistol as he did.

"Which way?" Von crouched beside him, shouting over the constant exchanges of plasma rounds and the clashing steel.

"Other side of the terrace." A hail of plasma peppered the wall, kicking up a cloud of white dust while Korso pointed towards a gated archway.

Nodding, Von swung his rifle over the wall, firing a long stream of rounds. "Go."

Korso took off, adrenalin fueling his legs, and vaulted over a bluish green hedge. Spotting a trio of soldiers ahead of him, Korso surged forward, shooting the first twice in the chest before catching the second with a knee. He unloaded a hasty round in the soldiers gut and turned towards the last soldier, but a round of plasma burned through the man's torso as Von caught up.

Sprinting over to the archway, Korso kicked the gate open and stepped into the marble hall—taking a moment to get his bearing's—and headed deeper inside, ignoring the roar of fighters soaring above and the ground shaking thud from AA cannons. The palace halls were surprisingly less chaotic than he would have assumed, save for the scrambling soldiers rushing to get outside or the occasional fleeing worker.

Dashing into a wide passage, Korso noticed a flash of silver light a second before Von cried out in pain, dropping his rifle.

Twisting around as he slid to a stop, Korso found a silver dagger sticking out of the T'loak's shoulder and discovered its source an instant later.

"Welcome to Ethria." Chaple stalked towards them, holding a second dagger. Eager to see the man dead, Korso raised one of his pistols, but to his surprise, Von stopped him.

"He's mine," Von growled, rage pouring from every inch of him, and ripped the dagger from his shoulder. "Find the Princess."

Korso started to protest but the burning look in Von's eyes warned him against it. "Yeah."

"As King of the T'loak, it is my duty to avenge fallen comrades." Von removed the spear hanging from his belt and extended it with a flick of his wrist.

Korso nodded, wishing him a silent good luck, then turned and continued down the corridor, desperate to reach Rachael.

* * *

Rachael stood clutching her bloody arm with a pained grin, taking in the carnage erupting outside. "Looks like Korso decided not to follow your script."

"How very clever of him." Cole continued to stare out the large tinted window, his knuckles turning white from squeezing his sword.

Rachael sneered again, reveling in the frustration in his voice.

A guard hurried into the chamber wearing a panicked look on her face. "My Lord, Enemy forces have breached the palace. I recommend…"

"Perhaps you should try killing them instead of wasting my time." Cole twisted around with snarl, lashing out with his sword and slashing the woman's throat.

"And you were having fun when you thought you were winning." Rachael glanced over at her sword, wondering if she could get to it and kill Cole before he turned around. "But it doesn't have to be like this. Kneel before *your* Empress and I promise you'll die swiftly."

"Death comes to us all in time." Cole turned towards her, antipathy burning in his eyes. "Yours is just arriving sooner than I had intended."

Cole lurched forward—his sword aimed at her throat—when a loud explosion blew through one of the walls, sending chunks of plaster and marble flying, knocking Rachael off her feet. Dazed with her ears ringing, she rolled to her back and froze. Rachael found the tip of Cole's sword hovering just above her left eye and swallowed, seized by terror.

"Cole!" Recognizing Korso's voice, a twinge of relief pushed against the torrent of fear stifling her breathing as she glimpsed Korso stepping through the large hole in the wall with pistol in hand. "Let her go."

"Throw away your weapons and she'll live." Cole adjusted his blade, pressing it against her neck. "Do it now, unless you came all this way to watch her die."

"This is between us." Korso tossed his pistols across the room reached for his sword, but as he did, another explosion blew out the tinted window, showering Cole in glass as he stumbled back.

Rachael reacted instantly, lashing out with a kick to Cole's chest before rolling to her feet. Scooping up her sword, she hurried over to Korso's side, ecstatic. "Took your time didn't you?"

"You sound like you missed me." Korso flashed a relieved smile. "I left the shuttle in the garden and the place is in chaos. You should be able to get to it if you hurry."

"What about you?"

"Cole and I need to talk." Korso returned his attention to Cole. "Go."

"Okay." Rachael nodded, realizing that she would be of little help at the moment, and backed away. "But you'd damn well better kill the tutin vastier. And don't keep me waiting."

Korso offered her a reassuring smirk. "Pushy Princess aren't you?"

Rachael smiled, running through the large hole and emerged in a smoke filled hallway. Making her way through the same corridor she had first ran into Korso, she veered left, moving closer towards the thundering battle outside. Rounding the corner to the next corridor, Rachael slid to a stop, spotting Lira standing over a dead T'loak soldier.

"What are you doing here?" Lira yanked her sword free from the soldier's chest.

"Get out of my way." Rachael glared at the woman, tightening her grip on her sword.

"I don't think so." Lira shot forward, attacking with a flurry of mid-level assaults.

Sparks flying with each collision of steel, Rachael deflected the incoming assault as best she could in spite of the aching lacerations inflicted upon her by Cole. Parrying a savage slash aimed at her head, Rachael countered, alternating from high to low swipes. Forcing the older woman back a step, Rachael went for another, however, Lira blocked the attack, retaliating with a kick to the stomach and blow to the head.

Reeling back while trying to suck air back into her lungs, Rachael whipped her sword to the right, hoping to catch Lira across the belly as she pressed forward but the Knight deflected her attack and swung high. Rachael ducked under the frenzied strike, but Lira caught her with a harsh elbow as she spun around and batted her sword away. Jumping back to avoid Lira's following swing, Rachael felt a surge of panic as she fell backwards, slipping on the blood pooling on cold floor.

Eyes wide, Rachael moved on instinct, scurrying back while Lira lifted her sword to finish her off and lashed out, kicking her leg out from under her. Lira fell forward, her head crashing into the wall while Rachael rolled clear of her blade. Pouncing on top of the woman, Rachael grabbed her by the hair, driving her face onto the tiled floor before scooping up her sword, rolling her over, and pressing it to her throat.

"Do you want to live?" Rachael sucked in air, her body aching as she held the sword.

Lira let out a painful groan, blood flowing from her nose. "Wha…"

"Do you want to live?" Rachael repeated, pressing harder on her neck. Waiting for Lira to nod, she leaned forward; making sure the knight could see the anger in her eyes. "Then you are going to do everything I tell you to, understand?"

"Yes."

"Good." Rachael lifted the sword and slammed the hilt onto the side of Lira's head, knocking her unconscious. Exhausted and aching all over, she slid to the floor and leaned against the wall, sucking in ragged breaths. "I need you to tell the galaxy a story."

CHAPTER ELEVEN

Korso stood in front of Cole, fighting back memories of childhood adventures and shared hardships. Through the destroyed window, he could see parts of the palace burning while fighters soared over head. The sounds of hundreds of pulse weapons discharging and swords clashing seemed somehow muffled as the two Ethrians stared each other down.

"Do you have any idea what you've done?" Cole began to circle around Korso, anger washing away his composure as his face grew red and lips curled into a snarl. "What this will do to the Empire?"

"I'm protecting Ethria, just like I've always done." Korso matched his movements, thumbing the release on his sword. "Just like you swore to do."

"I *am* protecting Ethria," Cole spat. "I protect her from fools like you; too shortsighted to see the future staring them in face. You fail to see the rest of the galaxy uniting under ideals we've always opposed. What happens when a united galaxy turns its sights on us? You and the Emperor would have left us weak and spent decades recovering from war while the greatest threat the Empire will ever know grows unabated. We have to strike first while *we* are strong."

"We won the war. The only threat left is you. You got so used to using fear as a weapon that you turned on our own people and conjured up a new threat."

"Spare me your petty judgments. They spring from a mind too meager to comprehend the shift in reality." Cole paused, gesturing towards the window. "You were the soldier the Empire needed before, but your time has passed. I am the ruler the Empire requires to survive."

"You seized power!"

"I had too! Someone has to do whatever is necessary to protect Ethria, but you don't see what I do. And since you can't and won't do what is needed, it had to be me." Cole's face hardened as he stood ready to attack. "I wish you were with me on this. You should be with me, but I will do whatever is required to protect our world, even if I have to bathe my sword in your blood."

Korso took a breath, readying his sword. "So will I."

"Make this easy. We've dueled before and I've won every time."

"Maybe, but I wasn't trying to kill you then."

"I will miss that inappropriate sense of humor of yours. Goodbye Korso." Cole sprang forward, intending to take Korso's head in a single strike, but Korso rolled under the attack.

Twisting as he rolled to his feet, Korso unleashed a flurry of rapid attacks, putting Cole on the defensive and driving him back. Switching from a high to low attack, Korso allowed Cole to parry his sword and nailed him with a harsh right hook. He twisted along with his momentum and directed his blade towards Cole's back with his left hand before twisting back around to strike at his midsection, however, Cole deftly blocked both attacks and batted his weapon downwards.

Surprised by the speed of Cole's counter, a surge of fear shot through Korso as he reared back, escaping a fatal blow by mere inches and raised his sword to block the following strike. Cole continued his assault, hammering away at Korso's defenses and producing a shower of sparks every time their weapons collided.

They both fought in a flurry of motion, evading and countering the other in a dance neither intended to lose. Ignoring a glancing cut to the leg, Korso went for a horizontal strike, which Cole managed to deflect and countered with a kick to the ribs. Taking advantage of the opening, Cole fired two swift thrusts, forcing Korso to jump back to avoid them, and twisted on his heel, driving his foot into Korso's chin with a side kick.

Fighting past the pain flooding through his head, Korso recovered in time to see Cole aiming for his throat and batted Cole's blade up and over his head. Cole repeated the same attack, but just as he deflected his sword, Cole spun around, aiming his blade at Korso's chest.

Korso leapt back, grunting at the sensation of cold steel slicing through his shirt and skin, adding to the collection of scars he had earned over the years. Anticipating Cole's follow up assault, Korso ducked beneath his arching blade and answered with an elbow to the face. Pressing his advantage, he hammered at his former comrades defenses when a large explosion rocked the palace, knocking them both off their feet and showering them with what remained of any windows.

* * *

Von rushed after the surprisingly maneuverable Chaple and swung for his head only to have his spear evaded yet again and a dagger almost plunged hilt deep into his midsection. Jumping back, he twirled his spear before thrusting it forward, and tried to readjust his aim while Chaple spun around the weapon, catching him with an elbow to the temple followed by a slash across his cheek. Snarling, more from anger than pain, Von lashed out while turning to face his agile opponent, and caught a boot to the face an instant before Chaple kicked his weapon free.

Refusing to allow himself to be killed, Von ducked and swayed to avoid Chaple's fluid series of attacks. Dipping under another swiping dagger, he answered with a shot to the stomach and followed with a swift punch to the ribs. Von pushed forward intending to tackle the older man, but Chaple was ready for the maneuver, gabbing ahold of him before twisting and throwing him over his hip.

Von landed hard on his back and rolled to the right, avoiding a dagger plunging towards his face. Not giving Chaple time to attack again, Von grabbed him by the collar while kicking his legs out, and spun him to the floor. Scoring with a pair of solid punches, he went for a third but Chaple blocked with one arm while driving a dagger into Von's thigh.

Pain shooting through his body, Von cried out and fell over as Chaple landed a fist of his own. He scurried to the right, with the dagger still in his leg, and dived to avoid Chaple's lunge. Feeling his hand brush against his spear, Von grabbed it—scrambling to his feet—and turned, striking Chaple hard enough across the face to knock the man back down and dent the metallic weapon.

Von pounced on top of the man, snarling as he drove the spear into Chaple's stomach, feeling it hit the floor beneath him. His breathing haggard, he grabbed Chaple by the hair and ripped the dagger from his bleeding leg before placing the tip under Chaple's chin with a slow, deliberate pace.

Fear lit up in Chaple's eyes as he struggled to free himself. "Please… mercy."

"No." Von pushed the dagger forward, keeping his eyes locked on Chaple's as he screamed and writhed in agony. Waiting until the dagger pierced the top of his skull, Von twisted it sideways before yanking it out with a grunt. "I will avenge my fallen comrades."

Driving the dagger into Chaple's already dead chest, Von forced himself to stand on failing legs and limped over to his pulse rifle. Fueled by nothing but sheer will and using the walls to remain upright, he started down the corridor Korso had gone through, determined to carry out his duties as King even if he died in the process.

* * *

Neither willing to yield to the other, Korso and Cole rolled to their feet, resuming their lethal ballet, too enthralled by resentment and ire to care about the destruction erupting around them or the pain racking their bodies. All that mattered was the dance.

They hacked and slashed away at each other, forgetting form and proper technique to attack with anything they could. Sparks flying as readily as their fists, Korso reeled from a blow to the jaw and countered with a low swipe, which Cole hopped over. He swung his sword to the left, intercepting Cole's while stepping back and maneuvered around a low sweep.

Cole continued his barrage with the intensity of a raging predator, forcing Korso back and sending tremors of pain rippling up his arms with every blocked strike. Slipping through an opening in Cole's assault, Korso caught him on the arm—eliciting a pained grunt even as Cole moved to counter—and unloaded a torrent of his own, putting Cole on the defensive.

Pressing his advantage, Korso shot forward, aiming at the center of Cole's bloody uniform, only to stab air while Cole twisted around the thrust and hit him with a harsh heel kick. Vision blurring, he felt a fresh wave of pain pulse through him as Cole thrust his blade into his shoulder while trying to spin away. Korso cried out, batting away Cole's latest assault and pushed him back.

His breathing labored and his body waning from loss of blood, Korso fought back the terror closing in on him and the darkness edging his vision. Looking over to Cole, he saw the same exhausted look on his face and searched for the friend that he had grown up with, fought alongside, and considered a brother, but that man was dead. Catching a haggard smile from Cole, Korso pushed aside his fatigue and returned his smile, realizing that their duel had reached its conclusion, one way or another.

Korso charged forward, meeting Cole's advance, their swords colliding in an eruption of sparks as they shot past each other. Twisting on his heel, Korso attacked; unsurprised that Cole had done the same, causing another cascade of sparks. Cole recovered first, attacking with a pair of frenzied strikes before scoring with a side kick. Staggering back, Korso parried a thrust and spun low, driving his sword into Cole's torso.

Eyes wide with disbelief, Cole fell on top of Korso, who lowered him to the floor, and grabbed him by the back of the neck. "Don't… settle in peace… protect Ethria."

"I will." Korso placed his hand on Cole's shoulder and tried to smile unable to forget the friend he grew up with.

"You'll… fail." Cole almost managed a laugh before his hand fell to the floor and his breathing stopped.

Slumping to the floor next to him, Korso stared up at the teal colored ceiling, growing more and more aware of his injuries. He hurt, more than he could have imagined a living person was capable of hurting, his pain emanating from more than just his physical wounds.

You'll fail.

Cole had spoken those words with a look of relentless abhorrence burning in his eyes that Korso knew he would spend the rest of his life trying to forget. However, at the moment, none of that mattered. His friend was dead. Rachael was safe. *Everything else can wait*, Korso thought before slipping into the darkness blurring his vision. *It's on her now.*

* * *

The morning sun shined bright over the imperial palace, which was still being restored after the battle to retake the planet weeks before. Hundreds of people, including holo-net reporters broadcasting around the galaxy, filled what was left of the blue-green lawn in front of the palace, intent on watching the events taking place under the elaborate banners decorating the burgundy arches that led inside. Standing beneath the arches wearing a long red and gold dress, Rachael addressed the sea of people, flanked by three imperial sages on her left and senior heads of state to her right, along with other important guests.

"What are you smiling at?" Korso glanced over to his right, where he found Dee grinning ear to ear. Both clad in their formal uniforms, they stood in front of the pack of statesmen while Rachael gave her speech. "We've been standing here for over an hour."

"I suppose I'm proud," Dee whispered in response. "I have known Rachael since she was a child, and now she is being crowned Empress."

"Shh." Lizabeth elbowed Korso in his side with her free arm while holding Von's hand with the other.

Still aching from his injuries, Korso stifled a groan, shifting his gaze towards his sister. "What? I'm just saying Von's was better. Succinct and to the point with much less ceremony is the way to go."

Von nodded, looking over the ornate surroundings. "I never did understand the Ethrian need for such pageantry."

"Neither do I." Korso laughed. "Part of our charm, I guess."

"Still…" Von smiled at Lizabeth. "I can get used to some Ethrian charm."

"I'm just glad this didn't turn out to be a funeral or something," Lizabeth stated. "Lucky that Lira woman helped clear your names."

"An impending death at the hands of a pissed off Princess tends to motivate one towards cooperation." Korso smirked, joining the crowd in applause as Rachael finished her speech. "Guess I'll have to start being nice to her now."

"Still pretending that you don't care for her?" Dee shot Korso a knowing glare.

"I don't," Korso replied, returning his attention to Rachael as she made her way towards them, pausing to greet any statesmen who approached. "Much."

"Of course." Dee stepped over to Rachael, along with Lizabeth and Von, offering their congratulations.

Fidgeting with his jacket, Korso followed a few steps behind them, smiling as he caught Rachael's vivid green eyes searching for him. "Congratulations, Empress."

"Thank you." Rachael returned his smile, her face a surprising shade of red. "For everything. I get why my father liked you so much. You're still a jerk, but, I see his point."

"I am going to miss these little sparring sessions of ours, brat." Korso laughed, noting that Dee and the others had joined Webber a few yards away. "So what happens now?"

"With our names cleared, we rebuild. Cole did a lot of damage, here and to the T'loak. Rebuilding alongside them is the best way to cement our alliance in the minds of our people."

"I meant, what happens now with us?"

Rachael looked away, acknowledging a senator as she passed by. "And what makes you think there is an us?"

"I seem to recall someone growing to appreciate my juvenile charms."

"And I seem to recall being labeled as mean and obscene." Rachael smirked, leaning in towards him.

"Yeah, but you're kinda pretty when you're pushy and obscene." Korso stepped forward, wrapping his arms around Rachael, and kissed her. Forgetting about the discomfort from his wounds or the crowd around them, he held their embrace, relishing the softness of her lips and the feel of her hand caressing his cheek.

"Finally," Dee muttered.

"Shut up." Korso shot him a brief look before Rachael turned his head back, resuming their kiss.

Pulling apart after a long moment, they both suppressed a nervous laugh—becoming aware of how much attention they had drawn—and joined Dee and the others. Despite the frenzy of questions being thrown at them, most coming from Lizabeth, Korso couldn't help but smile, enjoying the moment.